C.S. Boag is a former journalist who has also grown potatoes, driven taxis and bulldozers and worked in a hamburger bar. He has travelled many times throughout Australia and to France, speaking enough French not to die there. He was a Sydney City Councillor for six years and holds degrees from NSW and Sydney universities as well as postgraduate qualifications from Macquarie. Besides publishing short stories he has also worked as a columnist for *Woman's Day* and the *Bulletin*. He won the Walter Stone Memorial Prize for Literature in 1986. C.S. Boag lives on a small 'green' holding near Bathurst, NSW, with his wife, Judith. He has five children.

www.csboag.com

By the same author

The Case of the Hood With No Hands

The Case of the Death of a Ladies' Man

The Case of the Horses for Corpses

C.S. Boag

MISTER RAINBOW

in the Case of the

BULLETS AT THE BALLET

XOUM PUBLISHING

Sydney

 XOUM

First published by Xoum in 2014

Xoum Publishing
PO Box Q324, QVB Post Office,
NSW 1230, Australia
www.xoum.com.au

ISBN 978-1-922057-75-4 (digital)
ISBN 978-1-922057-76-1 (print)

Cataloguing-in-publication data is available from the
National Library of Australia

Word count 47,000

For my sister Annie

If music be the food of love,
you're in the wrong restaurant.

Chapter 1

THE KILLER ON CASTANET CLOSE

It's broad daylight – or daylight for broads, however you want to play it – and me and my one-legged mate Rory are busy at 21 Castanet Close turning over the place trying to find out where my ex-wife has taken our daughter. Aunt Rube is outside on the drive, checking the bins, removing bottles, cans, broken CDs, scraps of paper and fish heads and sorting them into piles marked:

Rubbish

For autopsy and

Clues.

Last time I looked, the *Clues* pile still had the VACANCY sign up.

Without warning, tinny music pierces the suburban quiet, and instinctively Rory dives for the gun he's built into his crutch, a nice little piece adapted to fire .45 hollows – slugs that don't leave the recipient begging for more. 'That's not Mr Whoopee!' he mutters. Rory might have turned Christian, but he's still a killer.

'Cool it, Roarer.' I go over to the window and peer outside. But he's right: the music isn't Mr

Whippy, it's the *Dance of the Sugar Plum Fairy* from Tchaikovsky's *Nutcracker* and it's coming from the little music box I gave my daughter Imogene when she still believed in fairies. Somebody's lifted the lid, but it doesn't mean we got to run around shooting ballerinas.

It's not like I wasn't warned. I lost count how many times Salina told me to clean up my act or she'd leave and take the kid with her. Now she's done it. They're not alone. It's written up there in neons, something Imogene said during the *Horses for Corpses* caper: 'Mummy's met a man she calls Mr Perfect – although she says after you *anyone* would be perfect ...'

And like Rube always says, perfect is as perfect does. The shack is as empty as the eyes of a killer just before he duffs someone. It's like the place has been given a pre-operative emetic and they not only removed all the dust, but the occupants' deoxyribonucleic acid as well. The kid's bedroom, the hall, Salina's bedroom, the lounge, the kitchen, verandah and Band-Aid-sized backyard are as bare as a pole dancer's belly. Even the light bulbs are clean. All bar the one that should be over the side door but isn't. Which confirms they're not alone. My ex never cleaned anything in her life.

I've already worked my way through the worst-case scenario – that Imogene was abducted – but there's no SOS (aka Signs of a Struggle), so she must have gone quietly. All that's happened, I keep telling myself, is Sal cleared out and took Immo with her. Just like she always said she would.

When the music box finally stops playing, Rube carries on with the sieving of the rubbish. Rube is the gumshoe aunt that took me in and set about teaching me the art of detecting after Dad dumped me. She's my safeguard against doubt. Rory's something else. Rory's a professional killer that found God but right now is a one-legged ball of anger stomping around the kitchen on his crutch-gun; like emotion ever solved anything.

'She took the kid!' He stops stomping and stares at his foot. 'It's ratshit, Rain.'

Rory's no Einstein so I keep the dialogue down around cellar level.

'I said cool it, Roarer. We don't know who this Lover Boy is and there's no big arrows telling us where they went. The only place we're going to find a clue is here – their last known place of habitation. So we got to do the search and we got to do it thorough.'

Roarer looks even more confused than usual. 'What are you on about?'

'I'm saying that while this might *seem* like an exercise in self-delusion, we –'

'I'm not talking about exercise.' He stomps his gun barrel on the swirly-patterned linoleum. It looks like the family dog just vomited on it.

'Like I said – it's ratshit.'

I need to have my wits about me – as opposed to half-wits like Rory – but he's a mate and his heart's in the right place, even if his brain isn't. Rory can always be relied upon to do the leg-work. As long as the leg-work only requires the one leg. I look where he's looking and see what he sees. Black pellets.

'They're just rodent droppings, Roarer.'

And the sounds outside are rodent sounds, like the ones in *The Nutcracker* when the Mouse King sets out to kill the dolls.

Rory does that thing with his forehead that suggests deep thought but is only the thing that Rory does with his forehead.

'Yeah, but they're getting up the barrel of my gat, Rain. And when that happens, my gat's –'

Suddenly I sense – no, I *know* – that something outside has changed. 'Hang on a sec.'

While Rory's been banging on about ratshit I've been half-listening to the orchestra outside – the wobbleboard of the Dixie bins, the *tap-tap-tap* of the timpani as Rube examines a tin, the wheelie-bin symphony of Rube going about the business of detecting. Which she's no longer going about.

'It's just that –'

'Roarer, shut up and listen!'

'But I can't hear anything.'

'That's just it, neither can I …'

The silence is broken by another *squeak-squeak-squeak* sound that might be rats, but isn't, and beyond that, the *tap-tap-tap* of sharp heels hurrying along the footpath.

I'm out of the kitchen like a shot out of Rory's crutch-gun, hat flying as my whitesides hammer the floorboards, a shoulder of my orange-fleck coat cracking against the door. I rip the .45 Taurus Millennium out of the holster as a shadow disappears through the hedge. Then I turn in the direction of the dry-retching coming from the driveway.

'Rube!'

Chapter 2
THE SOUND OF SILENCE

There's rubbish scattered all over the place, the music box is lying on its side and Aunt Rube's down for the count, the lump-knuckled fingers of one hand clutching the edge of a bin while the rest of her is face-down on the concrete, head twisted to one side, her skin fast acquiring the colour of what she's sprawled on. I hear Rory hoof-and-crutch it up the drive as I drop the gat and kneel beside Rube.

At first I think it must have been Pandora who got her, the nemesis that's been after me as long as I can remember. Pandora's neat and bloody-minded. But even as I think it, I know it's not so. *The knee bone's connected to the thigh bone and the doll dances only when you lift the lid.* Pandora clubbing Rube would be a coincidence. And I don't do coincidence.

Rory crutches back down the drive. 'What do you want me to do, Rain?'

I help Rube sit up while pocketing the music box.

'She's copped a thumping. She's got to be seen to. Get the Caddie, quick.' Rube groans as Rory heads for the wheels. 'Take it easy, okay?'

She shakes her head. 'I'm getting old, Rainbow. I taught you everything I know only to forget the basics myself. I was too intent on the rubbish. And he was quiet as a mouse. I should have been more alert. Hell, Rainbow, I was supposed to be helping you and then I go and do this.'

'You didn't do anything, Rube.' I cradle her head. 'Take it easy.'

'I have to help find the kid.' She knots her forehead, turning in on herself. 'I didn't see his face, just the hand. He was strong.'

'Jeez, Rube, if only I hadn't –'

Rube's voice cuts across mine like a scalpel. 'They were after *you*, Rainbow. I was just in the way, a pawn in a chess game in which the killer was after the King. He took me in passing. But something disturbed him. When he was laying into me I heard this squeaking sound …' She takes a shallow breath. 'Something spooked him. That's my impression, anyway. I know I taught you not to do impressions but …'

I hear the Caddie screech to a stop and Rube's light as pigeon feathers as I carry her up the drive.

'I telegraphed the hospital,' Rory says, holding the door open. I settle Rube in the back while Rory hands me a rug. I retrieve my coat, shrug it on and tuck the rug under Rube. Then I straighten.

'It didn't happen here, Roarer.'

'What?'

'Don't mention 21 Castanet Close. Don't say what happened or where. Rube fell while taking the bins out, okay?'

'You mean you want me to lie?'

'Only if it's not against your religion, Roarer.'

He hands me back my fedora.

'I'll do what God allows me to do.'

I shut the door on Rube as Roarer climbs behind the wheel. I got to trust him but it's like trusting a dingo in a chookyard. 'Drive like you got no licence,' I say. 'Imagine the car's nicked, you just robbed a bank and the cops are after you.'

Rory clunks the jalopy into gear.

'That's how I always drive, Rain.'

The name's Rainbow. You can spit on my card, bend it, twist it, rub it with your shirt sleeve or blast a hole through it with a .38, it will still read: Jack Black's Investigations. Whatever it says, I'm still Rainbow. The card's so I look respectable.

As I'm walking up the drive, Nosy Nora the next-door neighbour is on her porch, arms folded, head thrust forward into somebody else's business, her little shopping trolley sitting beside her.

'I was just coming back from the shops when I noticed …' she says, eyeing me like a snake watching its prey. 'Is everything all right, Mr –'

Nora's front gate requires something like a cast of the runes to open it. I kick it down and get up her path, fast. 'If the cops pay you a visit, Nora, you never saw nothing, understand?'

It comes out *unnerstand* and it comes out hard.

Nora shrugs. 'I been in the next-door neighbour game long enough to know how it works, Mr Whoever-you-are. But that doesn't make me blind and it doesn't make me stupid.'

'So tell me what you saw.'

'Well, I was just coming back from the shops and letting myself in the gate – which, incidentally, you'll have to get fixed …' Her eyes narrow to dollar signs. 'Was there something I *should* have seen?'

I lift her dolly cart and spin the wheels. They squeak. I put it down again.

'Did you see anyone leaving the premises dressed in, say, black?'

Pandora's favourite colour.

Nora shakes her head.

'I didn't see anyone. I was having trouble with the gate, so of course I wasn't looking anywhere else.'

'What about *before* you weren't looking?'

'I was shopping. And, oh my goodness, the price of food these days!'

I ignore the hint.

'In the days and weeks before you went shopping, did you see anything or anyone out of the ordinary?'

'What's it worth?'

'What's what worth?'

'My silence in the right quarters and my lack of silence right now.'

I feel the need to dramatise things but I keep it slow and breezy like we're discussing the weather instead of Imogene's fate.

'Lady, most people possess what might be called a *survival instinct*. Know why animals' noses twitch?' I lean in close so she can smell the threat and also so that my gat in its holster is clearly visible. 'Their noses twitch because they hear the hunter's cry, smell the cordite and see the dogs. They're not thinking about food or where their burrow is or the next tree to hide behind. It's more basic than that. All they want to do is survive.'

Chapter 3

WHAT THE NEIGHBOUR SAW

'What exactly are you saying?' Nora asks.

'You wanted to know what your co-operation's worth so I'm telling you.'

Nora takes a deep breath.

'All right, yes – I saw him.'

'The figure in black?'

'No, I'm talking about before.'

'Salina's lover?'

'I think of him as her regular guest.'

'And when did you see this "regular guest"?'

'When he was coming and going.'

'What was his name?'

'We were never introduced.'

'Describe him then.'

'I can't do that, either.'

I shake my head.

'Nora, for years you been hanging over your balcony, peeping around curtains and staring past your secateurs while pruning the camellias. Number 21 Castanet Close is your private stage and you got a permanent front-row view of the action.' I hunch forward again, let her catch another glimpse of the gat, and let her imagine what it might do to bilbies that don't talk. 'So describe the lover.'

Nora pulls her shopping cart between us. It's full of home-brand groceries. Nora knows the value of staying alive.

'I'm sorry but I can't. He came and went at night. There was no light in the driveway' – because Mr Incognito had removed the bulb – 'or I might have seen him. He was never more than a silhouette.'

'Use your imagination. You say *he*. Could it have been a *she*?'

'No.'

'Why not?'

'Because of the voice.'

It's better than nothing.

'Tell me about the voice. Was it low and murmurous or sharp and querulous? When he said hello to Salina in the darkness of the night and goodbye in the anonymity of the pre-dawn, did he do it *allegro*? Or did he do it nice and slow, like he had all night to say it in?'

Nora shakes her head.

'I can't say. But I *can* say that the voice had an unusual quality to it.' She does a *now-I'll-tell-you-the-truth* pause. 'I think he was foreign.'

It's not much but when you're desperate you settle for scraps. 'All right, on television, who did he sound like?'

She doesn't even have to think about it.

'Maurice Chevalier.'

'The joker in *Gigi*?' Nora nods. 'That's all you got? A silhouette that talks like a dead actor?'

'Yeah.'

'So when did they leave?'

'Just recently. A van took away the furniture. They left the same night.'

'And?'

'There's no *and*.' She's got her confidence back, the confidence that comes with knowing she's going to live. 'Unless, of course, you want me to start using my imagination.'

A nice old Indian V-twin with swept-back handlebars is parked outside the hospital. I like bikes, know my way around them, but I got to stick to the plan. Rory's waiting in Admission while Rube's in Ward No. 2 on the third floor wearing a back-to-front gown, her face as saffron as Mabel's in *The Simpsons*. In the room with her is a joker dying of consumption, a geezer in the last throes of double pneumonia, and a machine. I park myself next to the machine.

'Nice to see you're not dead, Rube.' She aims for a smile but it comes out a grimace. 'Have the cops paid you a visit yet?'

'I told the doctors I was dancing on the porch and slipped. They didn't believe me but at least they didn't call the cops. It doesn't mean they're not going to.' She nods at the machine. 'Meanwhile, they say that without Mr Dialysis here I'd be dead.'

There's something wrong with what she just said.

'People can live fine on one kidney, Rube.'

'That's what I've been doing since I was twenty.'

'What happened when you were twenty?'

'A bullet happened. The doctors had to remove one of my kidneys.'

After that there's total silence, apart from the croaking of the geezers and the thumping of the machine.

'Will it kill you to talk?'

'To the cops?'

'No, to me.'

Rube was facing north when her attacker punched her. The sun was in front, which meant that she didn't even see his shadow. 'There was a rush of cold air in the vicinity of the eleventh rib, just behind the peritoneum, to the rear of the abdominal cavity.' Rube grimaces again. 'It's like my assailant knew what he was doing.'

'You think he knew you only had one kidney? And you call *me* paranoid.'

'I'm not saying what I think, Rainbow, nor did I suggest you were paranoid. I'm just saying that's what happened. But he *might* have known about the kidney. These days, everything's in the public domain – phone calls, emails, hospital records, the works. *They* know everything there is to know about everyone.'

'So your assailant needn't have been someone you knew?'

'He didn't *need* to be. But that's beside the point. It wasn't *me* he was after, it was *you*.'

Back and forth and round about, like batting a square ball over a high net on a court without lines. I don't ask how she's sure, because she can't be sure. Her mind's been affected by the attack.

'I'm sorry, Rube. I shoulda–'

Rube frowns.

'Shoulda, Buddha! How many times must I tell you, Rainbow, that neither exists – neither *what might have been* nor a Higher Being. So don't let's have any of that malarkey about what should or shouldn't have been, don't let regret get in the way of –' She stops mid-lesson, cocking her head. 'Cops! I can hear them, smell them, taste their bile.' She nods towards a cabinet. 'The nurse put my stuff in that drawer. Open it.'

I open it.

'Now take out the purse and look inside.'

There's a ticket inside the purse.

'It was in the music box. The kid must have put it there.'

'Why would she do that?' I ask.

'I don't know, Rainbow. All I know is that Imogene must have thought it was important.'

Chapter 4
WHILE THE CAT'S AWAY

Rory's gone. He must have decided his responsibility ended when I turned up. I get myself home to the bashed-up old ferry I call the *Wooden No* (What's she called? nosey parkers ask. *Wooden No*, I reply). I then haul out Imogene's music box, place it on the chart table and prise open the tiny stage. Apart from the inner workings, there's one other item inside: Imogene's mini recorder, the one I gave her. The battery's dead. I take the battery out of my torch, insert it in the recorder, and switch on. There's the stuff Imogene recorded in the *Horses for Corpses* caper and after that a slice of the survival-ration German she's been learning – *Haben Sie ein Stuck Brot, bitte?* Then right at the end, a male voice saying one word. It's hard to make out. *Myrtle? Mater?* I turn my attention to the ticket, the one that Rube found. It's a child's concession to the ballet.

The *Wooden No*'s in much the same condition as Rube – dependent on a pump to keep her afloat. The bailing out takes an hour-fifty. Afterwards, I lie in the aft cabin staring out the porthole as the water works its way back in through the hole in the hull and the pump tries to work it out again. Just like I'm trying to work out the rat droppings at Castanet Close. The house was spotless. So why the droppings?

It's 3 am when I finally give up the struggle, grab the torch – along with bolt cutters, pliers and plastic card – unhitch the rowboat and row myself back to shore. After which I hoof it to 21 Castanet Close.

No-one's replaced the bulb over the side door. Why should they? Right now, the joint's a resident-free zone, containing no more than rats. I see what Nora saw. And that's all I see because my torch battery is in the mini recorder. But there's enough light to note that the bins are empty and the piles of junk have been cleared away. Which means I got a rat's chance of finding out anything via the rubbish.

I slip the plastic card between lock and flange and the front door swings open. The streetlights illuminate the bullet hole made by the psychopath that shot Imogene's three-legged cat, Tripodi, in *The Hood with No Hands* caper. The absence of the cat would account for the rats.

I get down the hall, through the living room and into the kitchen. I can't see much. But I know the water heater's a storage variety, 250-litre Rheem, the size and weight of a Rugby League front-row forward and about as moveable. There's fireworks when I cut the wires. After that, working by feel, I use the bolt cutters to cut the pipes. There are two – one top, one bottom, inlet and outlet, wet and wetter. Kneeling in the rat dirt, I fold the ends of the pipes and crimp them with the pliers. After that I do the Rheem dance, heel-and-toeing the water heater out of the corner. Rats like it hot and the hottest place in the house is behind the water heater. It's not only hot, it's also dirty. No-one cleans behind water heaters and Mr Clean was no exception.

My hand brushes against a bunch of hairless ratlets. It's a nest and I know I'm clutching at straws but I pocket a handful of the nest anyway. After that, I get the ratlets back in their corner, the water heater back in front of the ratlets and myself back to the *Wooden No.* And with daylight creeping over the horizon and a Manly ferry making too many waves, I sit at the chart table and dissect the contents of the nest.

Hair, toothless comb, scraps of cloth, a couple of feathers, shoelace, bits of plastic and a few scraps of paper. I check the hair. Salina's is peroxide-orange, Imogene's is a finer, tawny-coloured baby fluff, while Tripodi's – when he existed – was black. I find one foreign follicle. It could be significant but I'm not equipped to do hair.

I'm familiar with the threads worn by Salina and Imogene and the fibres in the nest match.

Using tweezers, I turn my attention to the paper: it's glossy and there are seven ragged pieces of it, some containing lettering. I get them all facing the same way. The piece with the capital letter *C* on it has a straight edge so I place it on the left. *Discard all preconceptions*, Rube always told me. *Don't force the pieces.* Rats are no respecters of words and in the end I'm left with five letters and too much chew. The magnifying glass reveals a bit of letter I've overlooked. It makes what I thought was a *C* into a

G. But is this one an *N* or an *M*? Is the *R* a *B*? Could the *F* be an *E*? That would give me a word: *RENCE* or *RECEN* or *CEREN* or even – *GREEN*.

The ferry returns, a green boat churning the green water white and shaking my concentration and the table. I slip the letters into an evidence bag and the evidence bag into my pocket. *GREEN* isn't much to go on, but at least it gives me a crypto-name for Salina's Lover Boy. Courtesy of the rats, I've got Mr Green. And courtesy of Imogene, I've got a ticket to the ballet.

Chapter 5

THE DANCE OF THE DEAD DOLL

The ticket's to the Big Sailbird, the Nun's Cowl, Three Sheets to the Wind – aka the Sydney Opera House – to see the ballet *Coppélia* tonight. No-one frisks me when I enter which means I go in armed but when a dowager bumps the mitt holding the tumbler, the beer splashes the gat and I got lager on the Luger.

The dame in the box office says my ticket is one of three booked in the dress circle, except the kid's ticket was cancelled. Less popular seats are still available – like the balconies along the sides, the loges – or she could sell me a seat in the front row, and that's the one I take. Aunt Rube brought me up on ballet so I could do pliés and demi-pliés, leaps, rolls, high dives and arabesques – moves that might prove useful to a detective – and I was taught dance by the great Madam Blavatsky, who trained a lot of those performing tonight. I'm still wiping beer off my jacket when I note a little man holding forth to a bunch of barely-pubescent neophytes agog with inattention.

'The under title of tonight's ballet,' the little man

says, adjusting his pink cummerbund, 'is *La fille aux yeux d'émail*. That's French for *The Girl with the Enamel Eyes*, a description I find so much more *apposite* than the one provided. Think about it – a girl with enamel eyes …'

The little man would like everyone to believe he picked up the voice in Aspen, Colorado, via Paris, France, and Eton and Oxford. But I can tell it's from Bullamakanka, just to the left of the Black Stump in the Back of Beyond.

'It's all about surrogacy,' he continues, looking around him. 'You know what surrogacy is, don't you, girls? Surrogacy is giving your life for others. In the ballet, the old man thinks he's bringing the doll to life but of course he can't.' The girls nod like they know what he's talking about. 'So you could call the ballet an allegory about man's arrogance …'

The bell goes for the first round and I head for the stalls. The rich get richer and they also get all the lookers. The figure on one dame isn't off the hook; what the brunette by the bar's wearing could be the Emperor's clothes, because there's little more to her clobber than the imagination; while the blonde with the unstockinged legs under a silver skirt fashioned from not much more than a pocket handkerchief is looking my way out of eyes a pulp-fiction writer might refer to as sloe: like the ripe, dark fruit of a wild berry.

'Come, come, Hélène,' says the old joker standing beside her. 'I'll take you somewhere afterwards.'

The ultra-riche – the take in the wonderful give-and-take that makes up Sydney society – are always more than willing to do something to their own benefit.

'I'm sorry but I'd prefer to go home,' the dame replies in an accent contemptuous of the aspirate. 'And by home I mean shame-wah.'

That would be *chez moi*, which is French for her own little truckle bed. And because she's looking at me when she says it, I'm half-thinking it might be me she'd like to go shame-wah with …

The only good thing about a front row seat at the Opera House is the leg room. Apart from that, you see far too much of the orchestra and also feel as exposed as the blonde with the silver skirt and the accent – a potshot for any sniper who might happen to be prowling the auditorium. I've got a view of the band, the legs of the ballerinas and the leg room. A hundred stall rows rake behind me, topped by the circle, and all the seats are full except those in the cantilevered boxes along the walls, which are empty.

You got to hand it to Delibes, the music's a knockout. The band does the prelude while the doll in the window stares wistfully at the revellers below. It's all swirling skirts, pink tights and boleros. It's great to look at but I'm not here for looking. This isn't some video on the laptop in the – all right, dis-comfort of the *Wooden No* – with the pump thumping in the bilge, a double whisky sitting beside me on the chart table and my finger on the pause button. There are no second chances here. There had to be a reason why Imogene hid the ticket. And if something happens, I can't just press rewind to find out what it was.

First insight: It's the band that are the automatons, not the dancers. What the dancers are doing isn't easy, it just looks that way. I know because I learnt ballet with a lot of these dancers.

Second insight: My ex-wife would have told Lover Boy I'm a private detective. Which means he would have known to cover his tracks. Hence the ultra-clean house. But why nothing from Imogene, except for a cancelled ballet ticket and a single word (Myrtle? Mater?) on her mini recorder?

The ballet dancers dance and the band plays and the sway of the music and the swirl of the tutus is as real as the rat droppings at Castanet Close. The old doll maker's given Franz a sleeping draught before dragging him across to the … *Him?* That's when I realise the production's traditional. And the tradition of *The Girl with the Enamel Eyes* is that Franz is a ballerina in travesty: the dancer's a dame. The hips are too wide, while the legs … Lisette Priée's too good a dancer for anyone to notice her gender, but now that she's in the arms of the old puppeteer and pretending to be male, I can see it. But then I stop seeing it. Because the puppet has risen from the dead and the music suddenly comes alive. As does Swanilda, pretending to be the puppet that's borrowed Franz's life and is launching into the 'Dance of the Dead Doll' while the old man clasps his hands and – *Crack, crack, crack!*

Chapter 6

CORPSE DE BALLET

No dancer's that good. Apart from which there's no stage direction saying that the old man's got to collapse, as far as I know. He's supposed to be over the moon because the doll's come to life, not –

Dead.

Final-curtain dead.

He's lying flat on his back and in death the years roll away to reveal a much younger dancer than he was pretending to be. I'm close enough to see his inferior maxillary drop and his fingers twitch and his body sag and the blood begin to drain from his arteries.

I'm right in front of the orchestra so a good part of my attention is on the violinists, bassists and bassoonists while the bad part of my attention is on the dancers. And none – I repeat, *none* – of the musicians was responsible for the noise suggesting the firing of an unsilenced pistol: no drumstick smacked against a drum edge or whip crackers making noises like fireworks. I know because I'm in the front row, with nothing between me and the band but a safety net.

There's a way onto the stage if you're prepared to

play it rough and I play it rough as I grapple-hand my way over the safety net. A big man in a rollneck is leaning over the dead dancer. Battered face. A pug. I flash a card. Any card. They never check.

'I'm from the police. What's the deal?'

'They got him.'

I ask the next question and I ask it fast.

'Who's *they*?'

The bloke doesn't answer. Instead, he says, 'It was my job to protect him and I stuffed it.'

'Who's *they*?' I ask again.

But I'm not going to get any sense out of him because he's a bodyguard whose CV's just been shot full of holes. I turn my attention to the corpse. And the corpse tells me the calibre of the bullets was .38 and at least two entered his head via the occipito frontalis region and exited via the coccyx.

Which makes it a loge shot – from somewhere up high in the balconies.

Someone's closing the curtains. The stalls are emptying. In the circle I spot an alluringly bare back framed in silver lamé. I shift my attention to the loges. They're empty. What did I expect? A nice man with his hands up saying, 'Arrest me'? I retire behind the curtains.

'Rainbow!'

She's a pair of shapely legs with a bulge in the crotch that doesn't go with the legs. It's Franz – or at least the doll that played him – a girl from Madam Blavatsky's dance squad who always tended to hang around long after the rest had left. Now rebadged as Lisette Priée, but once upon a lifetime ago, Jane Brown.

'Hi, Jane.' I indicate the body. 'Know anything about the *corpse de ballet*?'

Wrinkles spring into play about her eyes as she smiles, before she decides that undiluted joy at seeing me might be a bad look under the circumstances and plumps for abject sadness instead.

'Yes. Only, please, Rainbow – not here.'

We're standing on the eastern side of the Opera House with the tile-covered sails overhead. Jane shivers, hugging herself because no-one else is offering to do the job. Jazz floats up from a play boat weaving across the Harbour while the sound of sirens – cops, ambulance and fire – ransack the city. Jane's gnawing at her fist. Maybe she didn't have breakfast.

'I was afraid something like this might happen. Not a murder necessarily but still something bad. Sure, Simon had a bodyguard, but dancers can't take bodyguards onstage with them.'

She reaches down into her crotch and extracts the prosthesis that made her a male. I keep my eyes on her face.

'Why did this Simon joker need a bodyguard?'

Jane clutches the prosthesis.

'He and the lead dancer hated each other. There was even a punch-up.'

'Professional jealousy?'

She shakes her head.

'It was way beyond that.'

'So tell me about the hatred.'

'Why so impatient, Rainbow?'

'My kid's gone and I need to find her.'

Jane stares past me like she wishes she'd taken up tap. She's still got the misty-brown eyes set in an oval face she always had. And they still avoid mine like they always did.

'So you have a child now,' she murmurs. 'That must mean you're married – or as good as.'

I don't enlighten her. 'Jane, take away the frills and you'll find men aren't much more than what you just took out of your crotch. So forget your dreams, stick to the script and tell me what you know.'

Jane tells me that Simon Peter, the dead dancer, was a stand-in for the main drag.

'But why the hatred?'

'At first I thought it was an affair gone wrong. Then Simon came onto me so … Anyway, after that I thought it might be what you just said – a case of simple competitiveness. But it was more than that, a lot more. It was like Simon *knew* something about Janus that he shouldn't know and Janus didn't like him knowing so he was out to get him.' She pauses, fingering her prosthesis. 'It would explain the bodyguard.'

'Tell me about this Janus.'

'His full name is Janus King. He made a lot of money from dancing. But that's all I know. I'm a dancer not a detective.'

'So where is he now?'

'He was called away. Simon is – was – his understudy. Other than that I – I know nothing.'

She's no longer a boy, not even a ballerina. Just a girl I used to know who knows nothing except –

'I'm sorry, Rainbow, I wanted to talk to you. But what I've told you is the truth – Janus hated Simon and the hatred was due to something Simon knew.'

'How can you be sure?'

'The body language, of course. If dancers know anything, it's body language …' Her voice trails off, she lets her arms fall to her sides and somewhere deep inside the Opera House an orchestra starts up. 'And there was the bodyguard …'

'Where is he now – this Jason Robards or Janus McCoy or the Emperor Haile Selassie or whatever he calls himself?'

'Janus King.' The name's a match so I take it as a confirm. 'Like I said, he was called away.'

'Where to?'

'No-one knows.'

'Hazard a guess.'

'I suppose to Europe. Janus was – foreign.'

'Who called him away?'

She shakes her head.

'I'm sorry, Rainbow, but I'm just a –'

'Yeah, I know, you're a dancer not a detective.' Hoofs approach along the concourse, big hairy hoofs, the kind that usually belong to cops. 'They'll want you for questioning, Jane. You'd better go back.'

Lisette reaches out: an appeal for time to stand still, for a past that turned up out of nowhere only to disappear like the play boat that just crossed the

Harbour. But no-one can remake the past – not a doll maker, not a dancer, not anyone.

Chapter 7

THE FRENCH CONNECTION

Rube's still got a tube coming out of her and she's occupying a faded-blue hospital caterpillar chair while a dialysis machine thumps away beside her. Rory's brought her the *Complete Works* (*Complete Works of what,* Roarer wanted to know – *bridgeworks, roadworks, the kind of works you give someone when you ex 'em?*), her favourite pillow and her laptop.

'So who's this dancer you're after? And what's he got to do with the kid's disappearance?' she asks.

I tell her *Janus King* and that I don't know.

She nods and her tube nods along with her as she gets to work.

'The dancer, the dame and the kid all disappear about the same time,' she murmurs. 'So let's start with the name. According to Titus Livius – that's *Livy* to you, Rainbow, "Janus" means "gateway". That could be a *gateway of opportunity*. But Janus was also the god of two-facedness. As for *King* …'

She studies the screen, the eyes in the lined old face hooded with pain and the little body under the coverlet rigid. The stink in the ward is that of a public inconvenience on the cleaner's day off.

'What did the doc say, Rube?'

Her face is grey. It could be the reflection from the computer screen. Or it could just be grey.

'What doctors always say.'

'Would you mind elaborating on that?'

'Oh, you know, malarkey about a build-up of potassium and an inability to process waste. Expressions to make them feel superior; big words to justify their existence.'

'For Christ's sake, you're talking to me, Rube, not the janitor.'

She pauses and looks up. 'Rainbow, I'm shy a kidney and the one that's left has taken a beating. From now on my best friend's Mr Dialysis here. Do you want to know about Janus King or do you just want fairy stories?'

I tell her yeah, but she's not interested in what I was just saying, only in what she's reading, courtesy of some whacked-together public relations guff occupying the ether.

'Janus King was born Vladimir Gregorovich in the village of Petroville, the Ukraine, in 1986. It turned out he had twinkle toes. He came to the attention of the Russian Commissariat and was placed in the State Dance program, quickly graduating to the Bolshoi. He became premier *danseur*. But Vladimir still wasn't happy. So he defected.'

'He was quick on his feet then.'

Rube's crook so she lets that one pass.

'On his defection, Gregorovich changed his name to Janus King, joined London's Royal Ballet, and blah blah blah. Formed a relationship with a fellow dancer – female – and had a kid.'

I don't know why but I still ask, 'When was the kid born?'

Rube shrugs.

'It doesn't say. It just says he made a fortune out of ballet – it's possible if you're good enough. He joined France's Academie royale de danse from which he's currently on loan to the Australian Ballet.' She snaps the laptop shut and looks up. 'There's no mention of abandoning *Coppélia* but this is Wackipedia, not breaking news.'

Around us, the other hook-ups are in a state of somnolence. Some people get all the breaks while others just break. I don't know what category Gregorovich is in. All I know is I've got to find Imogene and the odds are lengthening. It's like Rube reads my mind.

'Ex-spouses take kids, Rainbow – it's what happens. You've got a headstart because you're a detective but you still need to sidestep your emotions. It's the only way you're going to find her. Stay calm and marshal your facts – and make sure they *are* facts – then do the deduction. Forget Imogene's your daughter and park any feelings you might have regarding Salina. Treat it like any other case.'

'I'll try, Rube. But just like you're my aunt and you're sick, Imogene's my daughter and she's missing.'

Rube reaches out a hand the colour of the stuff in the tubes and when it touches me it's shaking.

'I can look after myself but Imogene can't. I've lived most of my life but the kid's just starting. I'm pretty much dispensable but the kid isn't. So ...'

She takes her mitt away as a nurse arrives. They call them *sisters* now – no-one uses real names any more, it's part of the worldwide identity crisis. Rube waits for the pan-handler to leave before resuming speaking.

'So, stripped of emotion,' she says, 'this is what we're left with:

'Ex-wife disappears with lover

'The kid's with them

'Aunt Rube cops a beating

'A dancer is shot.'

She shifts the computer off her knees. 'Now tell me what you're *not* telling me.'

The paper forms a rough-cut daisy chain next to the words *PROPERTY OF THE NSW HEALTH DEPARTMENT* on the coverlet over Rube's legs. 'I'm sorry if I didn't mention this before, Rube, but you were crook.' I look at the letters. 'It spells *GREEN* if you use your imagination.'

'And if I don't use my imagination?' She shoves the paper aside with barely a glance. 'What then? Look, there are too many pieces missing. What else have you got?'

I don't like hospitals and Rube's too sick to be reliable.

'The neighbour said that Green – that's what I'm calling him – talked funny.'

'Her exact words being …?'

'She said he sounded like Maurice Chevalier.'

'That fat old bugger in *Gigi*? The one who sang about little girls?'

'*Thank heaven for little girls.* Yeah, that's the one.'

Rube nods. She's still not herself but she's more herself than she was before.

'Anything else?'

'Yeah, I found something in the music box – Imogene's mini recorder.' I take it out and press *play*. The word's still muffled. 'On reflection, it sounds like *mert*. It could be *murder*.'

'That would be the voice of our friend the lover, the one that the neighbour believes is French,' Rube says. 'If we go along with that, he's not saying *murder*, but *merde* – the all-purpose French swearword. Which means that – in the absence of evidence to the contrary – we can *assume* he's French.'

'But Janus King's not French, he's Russian.'

'All that means is that Janus King isn't our man.' Rube holds up a hand with the tube coming out of it to silence me. 'I know it's a long shot, Rainbow, but it's the only shot you have. You think rats chewed that paper because you're sure it wasn't a platypus, a kangaroo or a frill-necked lizard. All right, it's the same with Salina. Like most practical people, she's a romantic who would fly off to Paris at the drop of a hat. And that's what this case hinges on – romance.'

Rube senses my doubt.

'Look, I might be sick, but it's not my head that's affected. Nosy Nora the neighbour watches too much television but because of it she can pick an accent with her eyes shut. So if she says that someone's Maurice Chevalier, it means that person is French.'

I shake my head.

'In her last call to me Imogene said she'd had a medical and her photo taken for a passport.'

'That confirms the French option.' Rube sighs as she leans back. 'Does Salina speak French? Does Imogene?'

'No and no.'

Rube waves a tired hand.

'Well, then …'

It gives me something to do, anyway, at a time when I need something to do. At least I won't be twiddling my aquifers on the *Wooden No*. And it just might – I stress *might* – lead to something.

It's a long shot.

But like Rube says – apart from the bullet that took out the dancer, it's the only shot I got.

Chapter 8

C'EST MOI OR SAY NOTHING AT ALL

Out of the blue I get a call from Ace Mollema. I spent the first five years of my life with Ace on the Funny Farm – aka the hippy commune where our parents raised us in Nimbin, northern NSW. While I became a gumshoe detective, Ace joined the Australian Security Intelligence Organisation, commonly known as ASIO – Australia's equivalent of America's CIA. It's what happens to hippies' kids – they go off the rails. I tell him about Imogene. He offers to help and we arrange a meeting.

Sydney's premier clearing house for all things French is a glass-fronted joint in Sussex Street called the Alliance Française. A dame in Paris chic – high eyebrows, low hemline, acid glance – brushes against me as I push open the glass door. 'Oh, excusez moi,' she murmurs because she wants the world to believe that she's French. 'Merde!'

'Same to you,' I say as I saunter up to the guy at

the front desk.

'*Bonjour, m'sieur. Comment allez vous? Qu'est ce que c'est –*'

'In English, pal.'

'How can I help you?'

'I'm looking for a teacher.'

'Why do you want a teacher?'

'I want to learn French.'

'We teach French here.'

Salina's stolen the kid and, knowing Salina, it's an arrangement she wants to make permanent. That means she's got to hide her tracks. Which also means that if they took French lessons she wasn't going to be obvious about it. 'I want to do it like a consenting adult – in private.'

'*D'accord,*' says the joker behind the counter, like it's not *d'accord* at all but more like *Bugger off and stop wasting my time.* 'In that case, I suggest you consult the Sydney telephone directory. Or – on the off chance you've mastered the technology – the White Pages on the internet.'

I lean over the counter and my coat falls open. When in doubt, show them the gat. It tends to remove doubt.

'And I suggest you supply me with a list of private French teachers.'

He supplies me with a list of private French teachers.

Of the teachers on the list, one no longer exists, five no

longer teach, and the seventh is a funny little toe living in Bondi going by the name Jean-Pierre Boulevardier. He's got a French accent. They've all got French accents. Some of them even speak French.

'What do you want?' he says when I pay him a visit.

The door's open just enough to reveal a sloppy bottom lip and a suspicious eye. This is Bondi. It pays to be suspicious in Bondi. There've been a lot of muggings lately.

'I want to talk.'

'In French?'

'No, just talk.'

'I don't talk, I only give French lessons.'

I kick the door down.

'That'll do for starters,' I tell him.

The joint's the kind they dole out to people who would otherwise live in cardboard cartons and the man wringing his hands would come into that category long before he'd come into anything else. He's wearing a decade-before-last T-shirt, a crumpled set of underdaks and a scared face.

'I'll call the cops!' he squeaks.

I shove him back into the room that's just this side of being a box.

'And what are you going to call them? *Messieurs? Gendarmes? The Boys in Bleu?* Or just plain busy. Because that's what they'll be, pal, and they won't appreciate being bothered by someone with a fake accent, dirty underpants and no observable means of support. So shuddup and siddown.'

He shuds up and sids down, giving me the chance to appreciate what a fake French teacher looks like on his day off. 'What do you want?' he asks.

'Information. Starting with the identity of your students.'

'That's private.'

'That's good because I'm a private detective.'

The stench of boiled cabbage and mould wafts through the doorway behind him and the traffic on Bondi Road is as calm as a tsunami.

'Show me some ID to prove who you are,' he says.

'I've got a better idea. You identify your students, thereby proving you want to stay alive.'

I've discovered most people want to stay alive, even ones with fake French accents, soft hands and jowls like badly-set jelly. He climbs to his podcasts, drags himself to an old desk, digs in a drawer and produces a notebook like he's surprised to discover it's there. Holding the book at arm's length so I don't get the plague, I pick my way through the sex shops, wanking salons and spiderweb sites until I find what I'm after. I stab my thumb at a name.

'Describe them.'

'Describe who?'

'It says here: *Smith.*'

He describes someone that couldn't be Green, Salina, Imogene, or even Janus King. After which I walk him through the rest of the names. The second from last's a possibility – two adults and a *skid.*

'Got a mobile number for them? Email? An address?'

'They didn't provide any contact details.'

'So give me a description.'

He gives me a description and it's not them. I chuck the book back at him and tip my fedora.

'I won't trouble you again. Unless you trouble me first.'

'How how might I do that?'

'In any number of ways but primarily by going to the cops.'

'I won't go to the cops.'

'If you're ever tempted, just remember the Bondi mugger.'

'Who's the Bondi mugger?'

I pick up the door and lean it against the architrave.

'C'est moi.'

After that there are another fourteen futilities. But I don't give up. And it's good I stay with the program, because on the fifteenth go I strike gold.

Make that silver.

Chapter 9

A DAME CALLED DAMNATION

'Why, hello there.'

She's still blonde, she's still beautiful and she's still looking at me out of the same sloe eyes she had at the ballet – only now they're sloer. Her modesty's no longer in danger from the scrap of lamé, but it's a fair bet the khaki affair she's wearing doesn't possess a back either. She's got an accent that's genuine French and I've tracked her down to an immodest four-up, half-a-dozen down, full-brick-and-tile Edwardian mansion in upmarket Mosman. To cover my contusion I pretend to tick a name off the list I got from the bloke in Sussex Street.

'Would you be Hell and Damnation?'

The dame with the eyes nods.

'It's Hélène, actually.' She throws me a glance I could only describe as winsome – or appealing, or lovely, or knee-trembling. 'And it's Dalmation, not Damnation. Which makes my appellation Hélène Dalmation, rather than what you just said.'

Whatever it sounds like, she'll always be Hell and Damnation to me. I get a grip on her mitt – it's more than I got on myself – and her skin feels like the inside of a dream. I check if she's wearing gloves but her hand's as bare as my emotions.

'I'm Harry Golightly and I'm a dick.' It's not how it was meant to come out so I try again. 'What I mean is that I'm a private detective and we need to talk.'

She opens the door and my heart – or whatever I got thrashing around in my ribcage – goes arrhythmic enough to earn me a bed next to Rube's.

'I think you could do with a drink,' she says, crossing to the expensive-looking liquor cabinet under an even more expensive-looking Picasso. She pours a couple of drinks out of an expensive-looking bottle and I see that I was right. Her dress doesn't possess a back, her beautiful neck rising out of her *scapulae* like a lily out of a pond by Cezanne. She hands me a glass as big as a bidet and sits in a couch that didn't come from Ikea before fixing me with a look and murmuring, 'Haven't we met somewhere before? You look familiar.'

She's brought the bottle with her, she's sitting far too low in the couch for comfort – mine, not hers – and the wine is late-cut Beaujolais.

'You were at the ballet with your grandfather,' I reply. 'So was I, but without the grandfather.'

When the dame laughs, she reveals a set of teeth almost good enough to go with the eyes.

'You say the cutest things, Mr Private Detective.' She wipes what might be tears of mirth out of the amethyst eyes with one of the hands that aren't wearing gloves. 'Yes, I was at the ballet, but not with my grandfather. His name's Albert Flax, he's an ex-Olympian and rather wealthy.' She notes the direction of my glance as well as that of my thoughts.

'French lessons couldn't pay for all this, could they?'

'I don't know, could they?'

The sloe eyes change shape like an amoeba.

'I remember you now. You're the man who leapt onto the stage after that ballet dancer was shot.'

I'm not so far gone that I don't know an inconsistency when I hear one.

'How do you know he was shot?'

The reply comes back as smooth as the Beaujolais.

'Why, it was all over the media, social and otherwise. I should have thought that a detective would keep up with the news.' She crosses to a magazine rack and the afternoon sun gambols in her hair.

'This is what one paper said.' Her beautiful hands flip the pages. '*Dance of Death. A young man playing an old man became a dead man last night when …*' She palms me the blatt. 'You read it, I can't bring myself to.'

While the dame resumes her perch, I wade through the purple prose. It doesn't tell me anything I don't know already, except how the dame knew the cause of death. Her hand brushes mine as I hand back the paper. I want to trust her, and because of the hand-brush I want to trust her even more.

'So what's your interest in all this, Mr Private Detective?'

It's like I'm hypnotised – or maybe it's the wine or what I just read in the blatt – but I tell her. Not everything, just enough to give the impression that

I'm open without spilling my guts; enough to endear myself without compromising my integrity; enough to set the stage for any *pas de trois* that might await Hell, me and Damnation in the future.

'Well then,' she croons softly after my spiel, and the amethyst eyes switch to mauve, 'how can I help?'

'You teach French,' I manage. 'And I thought you might have taught my ex-wife and daughter.'

'Why would they want to learn French?'

'Because I believe that my ex-wife's lover is French. Also because I've got nothing else to go on – apart from the crackpot ideas of a sick aunt and the sad hunch of a bereft father.'

'But why me?'

'Because you're one in a million.'

'There aren't a million French teachers in the world.'

'What I mean is that I've interviewed a lot of French teachers and you're the last on a very long list.' I hold up my glass. It's empty. 'So did they?'

'Did who what?'

'Did my daughter and her mother come to you for French lessons?'

The look she gives me is like the one she gave me at the ballet. During which she takes a deep breath and at the same time seems to come to a decision.

'I'll need a description.'

'No, *I'll* need a description. As well as a list of your students.'

'I'm sorry but I'm discreet.' She considers me for a moment. 'But I suppose that needn't prevent me describing my students.'

It's a long list – she'd be a good teacher if only her

students could concentrate on the lessons – and it's a long while before she gets to Salina.

'She's a woman who speaks her mind but is still quite pretty, in a hard sort of way.'

That's Salina, or a close approximation of her. It's my turn to lean forward but I keep the gat covered.

'Did she give you a name?'

The dame shakes her head.

'Not one worth knowing.'

'Describe the kid.'

'A sweet girl who picked things up quickly. She quite liked ice-cream but was somewhat perturbed as to why she needed to learn French.'

'In what way was she *perturbed*?'

'I overheard her asking her mother why they were here.'

'And what was her mother's reply?'

'She said it would be a shared interest.'

'That's it? She told the kid they were *bonding*?'

The dame shrugs. 'Correct. But I sensed the girl didn't believe her. She kept quiet.'

That's Imogene. And the liar had to be Salina. But I already know Sal and the kid. It's this dame that I'd like to know better.

'What about the man that brought them here?'

'He stayed in the car; I never saw him. He just dropped them off then picked them up afterwards.'

If I had a description of Mr Green I'd be closer to finding Imogene but all I've got is a foreign accent and a word. It's a dead end. I thought I might have struck gold but it's only Grade 3 dross. Our hands don't touch as I return the glass and the reason for that might lie in the dame or in me or in both of us.

'Thanks. I won't need to trouble you again.'

'I like you,' the dame says slowly. 'So while I might not be able to describe the man, I *can* describe his car. It was a hire car and it came from those people with the inexplicable and possibly sexist motto: NO BROADS. You know, I've always wondered what that actually means ...'

And I wonder about the dame as she follows up with the dates and times of the visits, and the beautiful smile has just become that much more beautiful as she sees me out.

'Just now you said you wouldn't trouble me again,' she says as her hand finds mine. 'But did you ever think I might like to be troubled?'

'What about the ex-Olympian?'

The beautiful smile changes to an even more beautiful grimace.

'Albert's really more like a ... grandfather figure to me.' The hand lingers in mine. 'So let's not say goodbye but *à bientôt*. Or in English, don't be a stranger.'

Chapter 10

GIVE A MAN
ENOUGH ROPE ...

A lot of detecting is just standing and waiting and I stand and wait at the car-hire place until the blonde with the kohl-ringed eyes and the plaintive soul lets herself out via a side door and trots off into the night examining her fingernails. When she's gone, I pull on the rubber-duckies and go in.

The security's the kind that companies install to satisfy the insurance. Apart from the insecurity, a cement apron contains a bunch of cars bearing the words *NO BROADS*, there's a glass-fronted office and a sign in the window says *NO CASH KEPT ON THE PREMISES*. I punch out the CCTV, check for trip wires and climb in the window the blonde left open in return for money to fix her fingernails with, plus a little left over for her toes.

Once inside, I flick down the blinds, adjust the ex-army torch to high beam, drag the paper serviette out of my jacket, and settle myself at the big black Dell computer in the corner. It's not easy fingering a keypad with gloves on but after a few mis-taps, I manage to enter the security code the blonde wrote on the serviette which gets me *LOGBOOK*, followed by *whorentedwhat*, which gets me the rest.

I hit *SORT BY DATE* and after that I key in the data provided by Damnation. Traffic hums, neon lights flicker, a dog barks and the desktop eventually coughs up a name. *Xylophanio Xalades.* That's a name? I key in the dates again, blink in the neon, and switch my attention back to the computer like I might surprise it into telling me the truth and the truth might be different to what it's already told me.

But the name's still Xylophanio Xalades and the joker must have used it for the same reason I wear flash clobber and a hat. Because long after what a witness sees is overtaken by sports scores, that's all they remember – the funny name, the fancy clothes and the hat.

I ask the computer for the licence and when I hit *print*, the machine at the other end of the counter spits out a head-and-shoulders of Xylophanio Xalades, who might also be Mr Green – the joker that Salina fell in love with enough to run away to God-knows-where with my daughter.

It's been decades since we've seen each other, so Ace Mollema's little more than a memory. But he's also an outline in an unlit room, his voice roughened through shouting passwords to strangers while arresting enough terrorists to justify a budget that would support a minor royal.

'How've you been, Rainbow?'

I strain to hear him over the background music

– which is on loud because the safe house might be bugged – and nod before realising Ace is in the same position as me, and just like he can't hear whispers, he can't *see* much, either.

'I'm fine,' I say. 'Did you bring a computer?'

I figure he must have nodded because there's a nod-length pause. After which he adds in a voice that only just makes the high-jump over the music, 'Plus a scanner and a printer.'

Seen from the road, the safe house could be an electrical sub-station. It's designed to look like a house without actually being one – a non-address in a non-street in a non-suburb that wouldn't even show up on Smoogle Earth, and the music's Beethoven.

'I hear of you from time to time,' Ace says, the glow from the laptop illuminating his shirt, but not his face. 'You're under everyone's radar except ours. Because we know everything. I remember when we used to play cops and robbers – we thought we knew everything then, too.' Pause. 'And, of course, I'll never forget what you did.'

'All I did was get you out of a hole, Ace.'

The computer screen flickers and beyond the Beethoven I can just make out the sound of Ace's mastic gloves on the keyboard, followed by the cheese-grater rasp of his voice. 'I remember like it was yesterday. You were pretending to be a cop while I was a robber on the run when I fell down that shaft. Hippies don't think about kids falling down mine shafts, they're too busy being hippies. But you saved me.' I shrug before remembering that he probably can't see shrugs.

'We were mates.'

'And of course we still are.' It's a spy's voice but I've got to trust him; there's nowhere else to go. 'How could we not be,' the disembodied voice continues, 'seeing that I owe you?'

I don't do the shrug, just raise my voice enough for him to hear me over the music.

'Yeah. And now I'm the one in a hole.'

'And it's my turn to provide the lifeline. What do you need?'

'A temporary passport.'

There's no hesitation. 'We can do passports.'

'It's got to work but no-one can know it's me,' I continue. 'I'm a non-person. I haven't got an identity, and if I didn't need a passport real bad, I wouldn't be asking for one.'

'Okay, I'll have to guess what you look like,' Ace says, 'based on no more than the remembrance of things past. And after that, find a match among the passports of dead men.'

'Can you do that?'

'Consider it done, Rainbow. And after it's done, consider it forgotten. Now is there anything else — apart from the passport of a dead man who looks like what I think you look like after forty years?'

'He's got to be bald.'

'We can do bald. Anything else?'

I reach across the space between us, find his gloved hand with my ungloved one, and palm him the picture from the hire-car joint.

'If you know everything about everyone, tell me who this is and where he went.'

'No problemo.'

The stereo churns out *Song of Joy*. I like *Song of Joy*. It's not just the words. Music says stuff you can't put into words.

Like vain hope in the face of impossible odds, confronted in darkness.

Chapter 11

... AND HE'LL HANG HIMSELF

Like Ace says, the spy boys – CIA, ASIO, Mossad, the KGB and the New Zealand Tomahawk Club – know everything there is to know about everyone and then some. I don't like dealing with them but sometimes there's no choice. If I'm going to find Imogene I've got to use every resource I can lay my hands on.

I saved Ace's life when we were kids. That's got to count for something, even to a spook. So after leaving the safe house, I find a nearby café, order an espresso, park my suspicions and study the paperwork. Ace has come up with three starters, each face an inverted triangle, eyes so far apart they might have come from broken homes, and all of them handsome. Salina is a great judge of character – all they got to be is handsome. I suppose that's where I fell short – I look like the backside of a bookcase.

Mr Green no. 1: Real name, Bruno Foxx. Unlikely name, unlikelier person. An orphan, he was fostered young. Ungrateful little bastard proved incorrigible. Finally rejected by his ultra-kind and ultra-peace-loving foster family. After which, in and out of reform school. After which again, in and out of the slammer; offences ranging from taking things that didn't belong to him to attempted murder. When not in jail, a drifter. Believed dead, but you believe what you want to believe in this game.

Mr Green no. 2: Real name, James Hamersley. Single child. No bright spark but apprenticed to an electrician. Married, founded his own business. Became a local politician in the staid backwater where he and Mrs Hamersley set up house. Pillow of the community. Two children and a mistress. Awarded an order of something, the kind that only money can buy. Hypocritical, but I can't let my feelings influence my judgment.

As I wade through the paperwork, Imogene seems further away than ever. That's the trouble with desperation – you leap from one long shot to the next only to end up in the Glebe Morgue. I take stock: there was Rube's mugging, a ticket to the ballet, a death and a voice on a mini recorder. One of these jokers is Lover Boy. Pigs fly. I take a swig of the swill. Talking of pigs, you wouldn't feed this muck to them.

Mr Green no. 3: Serge Lifar. Where would anyone get a name like that? The dossier doesn't say. What the dossier doesn't say interests me. Lifar appeared out of the blue – or rather black, because that's the colour of the ink hiding his origin and just about everything else about him. He attended *blacked-out* university where he studied *blacked-out* – six letters or maybe eight. A succession of girlfriends, nothing permanent, *names deleted*. I check the picture. He's even prettier than the other two. Became *blacked-out* to various *deleted*. Deregistered as a *blacked-out*. Involved in *deleted* enterprises. Assisted in (see file *blacked-out,* not attached). Currently *deleted*.

There's something wrong here. I climb out of my comfort zone, leave the café and head for the station. All of a sudden there's no time for comfort zones.

The off-white car with the mud-spattered and therefore unreadable numberplates sidles off into the streetscape as I board the train. There's no need to follow trains. Unless they go off the rails they always end up somewhere unsurprising. And there's no-one tailing me when I alight from the carriage at Central. But I'm not looking for tails. I'm too busy trying to work out where Salina took Imogene.

That and the *blacked-out* background of Lover Boy.

It's raining, Rube's been discharged, she's back home and she's got company – a great throbbing lump of a machine next to the day bed in her inner-city hovel. Coffee's bubbling on the rusty Porta-stove while Rube's hooked up to the machine by the usual tubes and gazing up at me, whey-faced.

'I've renamed the machine Mr Heartbreak.'

I rescue the coffee, fill a cup, pass it to her, and she accepts it with shaking hands.

'So how long's Mr Heartbreak going to be around?' I

ask, pretending not to notice the shaking hands.

The coffee spills and the planet teeters on its axis. First Imogene, now Rube. She waves the hand that's not spilling the coffee like she hasn't a care in the world, even if she's only got one kidney and it's fried.

'As long as I want to stay alive, Rainbow.'

'You mean *forever*?'

Her eyes slew away and when they come back to me, she's still trying to make them look calm.

'Of course not. Just a couple of hours every couple of days. But enough about me.' She points to the papers. 'What have you found out?'

After I've filled her in, Rube's nodding. It might be because some of the pieces are falling into place. Or it might be because she's falling asleep. 'Anything else?' she says, opening her eyes.

I look out at the rain and when I look back I'm frowning. 'I'm worried about you, Rube. Other than that, I'm worried about Imogene, I'm worried about Pandora and I'm worried about Ace – I don't like him knowing who I am.'

Rube smiles.

'I can look after myself – always have, always will. As for the rest, Pandora wasn't the thug who biffed me and the spy people know little or nothing about you – I took care of that long ago. Your birth certificate disappeared and you've got no health records and no identity card. You own no property, nor do you have any kind of licence. The marriage and divorce papers are gone. As far as the world's concerned, you don't exist. One fake passport's not going to change that.' Her bony hand lights on mine like a shadow. 'So tell me what else you have.'

'After Ace produced three possible identities for our Mr Green, I asked him to cross-check Imogene and Salina against outgoing air traffic.'

'Does he know where they went?'

'Their departure cards agree with you – Paris.'

Rube taps the papers.

'And which of these Mr Greens is Lover Boy?'

'Serge Lifar ticks all the boxes. He's pretty so Salina would go for him. He's also a crook, but ASIO's protecting him, so I'm guessing he's helped them in some way. He'd be a convenient passport for Salina. She wanted to take the kid and he was her escape route. She knew I didn't have a passport. What she didn't factor in was that I knew Ace and that Ace could get me one.'

Rube shakes her head.

'Rainbow, I can't help on this case.' She lifts an arm and the tubes with it. 'I'm a prisoner of this stupid machine. Worst of all I'm in a negative space emotionally. So you're on your own.'

She closes her eyes then opens them again.

'What about your profile? Who are you taking with you? A sister? A wife?'

'At this stage it looks like I'll be travelling alone.'

Rube's known me since I was a kid. She looks out the window. The rain's bouncing off the rooftops and forming a fine mist on the tar macadam.

'I understand, Rainbow. It's a case of the less I know the better, isn't it?'

Chapter 12

INNOCENCE AND ERMINE

I'm wearing T-shirt, jeans, purple sneakers, hip gun
– a nice little .25 Browning Stubby – and I'm fairly
sure I haven't been followed. But you can never be
certain of anything in this game. For my money –
whatever Aunt Rube says to the contrary – Pandora's
still a suspect. I've got a bad feeling but I'm used
to bad feelings. The Rolls-Rorters, Lexi-Cons and
Mercy-Dies sidle between me and the mansion. I
got here before lunch and now it's late afternoon,
a classless wind dragging the ordure of the hoi
polloi across the Harbour while expensive sunlight
glimmers off the broad-acre swimming pools of
God's favourites.

You can't help the odd idle thought while
surveilling – like death it comes when you least
expect it. That doesn't mean I don't keep my eye
on the doorway of No. 31 Exemplary Parade while
relieving myself in a corner of a garden that might
have been modelled on Versailles.

She turns up at six. Even in a black suit and carrying

a black handbag, Hell and Damnation's still milky-skinned, blonde and knee-knockingly beautiful. I allow fifteen minutes for me to calm down and Damnation to make herself comfortable before rapping on her front door. When she answers I try my best to keep it casual.

'I was past justing and thought I'd good in to say call by.'

She's taken off her day clothes and donned a bathrobe that reveals too much of her to make anyone but herself comfortable, while the tips of her soft hair caress her shoulders and her eyes have got too much violet in them not to be dangerous.

'Oh, it's you,' she says and smiles. 'I was just about to take a bath.'

'Where were you going to take it to?'

The smile turns into outright merriment.

'Why, that's so *clever*, Mr –'

'Call me Rain. That's what my other friend calls me.'

'*Reine?* As in *Queen?*'

I shake my head. It helps to clear it. Not completely, just enough so I can answer.

'No – *Rain* as in *Spain*.'

The dame barefoots it back towards the hallstand and her smile goes all the way down to her toenails.

'I notice,' she says sweetly, 'that you said your other "friend", in the singular. I couldn't help wondering: would that be a male or a female friend, in the singular.'

'Yeah,' I tell her and the bottom of her bathrobe flaps a merry little welcome as she lets me in.

While the bathtub's making the kind of noises bathtubs make when they contain dames, I search the house, starting with the bedrooms. I can't move the furniture or she'd hear me over the bubbles, so I feel behind the wardrobe for the hidden safe, get down on my knees to check under the bed for the biscuit tin containing the C-notes, and scratch through the jewellery box for jewels that are far too expensive for a teacher – even one supported by a wealthy ex-Olympian.

But there's no hidden cash, no secret backs to the drawers and no observable skeletons in any of the cupboards. So I go back downstairs and take a gulp of the whisky so she'll think that's all I've been doing. That, and admiring the pictures of the French castles in the magazines she left me along with the whisky.

After that, I check out the rest of the house, starting with the scullery. Inside the sugar bowl, on top of the cupboards, under the freezer, behind the stove – all the obvious places. Followed by the not-so-obvious places. After which, I search the living room containing the Picasso with too many eyes in it, followed by the study. Always with an ear to the bubbles plip-plopping and the body slip-sliding to make sure the dame's not where I don't want her to be. At least not until I've finished my search.

But the dame's clean. Or as clean as any dame can be that's just taken a bath and is now standing in the bathroom doorway, wrapping herself in a bathrobe and calling out, 'Where are you?'

She's expecting me to be in front of her when I'm behind her, that I'll be in the living room when I'm in the sunroom, and that if she stands in the hallway covering her front with her bathrobe, she'll avoid exposure. I catch a rear view of a beautiful thigh and I'm wondering what else she's trying to cover up when she turns and catches me wondering.

I quickly drain the rest of the J&B.

'I'm here minding my own business. Plus whatever else happens along that might need minding.'

Her face has turned a deep shade of pink. I can't speak for the rest of her because she's finally herded herself back into the robe.

'I – didn't expect you to be – where you are,' she says.

I shrug. 'Neither did I.' I hold up the glass like a shield. 'But I've completed my tour of the whisky and was looking for more.'

The dame's no longer smiling.

'I'm not in the habit of storing drinks in the hallway. Also –'

But I don't hear the *also*. The double-report of a gun followed by the sound of glass shattering and the noise of a rapid departure puts paid to that. I hit the carpet, taking the dame down with me. When I get back to my feet and into the living room, the Browning's in my fist and the first thing I notice is the broken window; the second is that the Picasso's got even more eyes than it had before; and the third is that there's no glass on the floor.

'Wh – what ...!' cries the dame, trying to keep

her gown closed while at the same time keeping her beautiful eyes wide open.

'Stay down!' I yell.

Damnation stays down and I get myself into the garden. The sun has set on the expensive carriageway and there's nothing left but street trees, muted orange lamps and glass on the grass under the window. No sign of any shooter. I come back and check out the dame. She's tied up the bathrobe. I garage the gat.

'You got any enemies?' I ask her.

'No. Have you?'

I busy myself rechecking the window, followed by the painting. And after that, the frame around the painting and the wall around the frame. There's enough lead to make an anchor for the *Queen Mary*, yet the pellets form no more than a six-inch spread on the wall.

'Know anyone that could shoot that good?' The dame shakes her head like she doesn't understand the question. 'Okay, go and change into something more uncomfortable while I clean up. We'll both feel better that way.'

While she's gone I check her handbag: keys, powder, lipstick, eyeshadow, wallet. Her driver's licence contains the face of a dame with sloe eyes and the name reads like it's supposed to read. There's a Medicare card, health insurance plastic and a library voucher – all the ID other people possess but I don't. An electricity bill proves she lives here. A couple of hundred bucks prove she's not broke. And a passport proves –

The traffic's dying but I don't want to die along with it. I step to the front door and rip it open. Nothing. I close the door and tippy-toe to the base of the stairs. From above comes the soft sound of bare feet and the noise of drawers opening and closing. The shells on the floor are Winchester 12-gauge SSG. I return to the handbag and examine the passport and by the light of the hall sconces make out the following:

The passport's current

The ID in the passport matches the one on the driver's licence

The dame likes travelling from Sydney to Paris and back again.

The sound of espadrilles fluttering down the stairs gets the passport back in the wallet, and the wallet back in the bag. I turn around and there's Damnation standing before me, all clad in innocence and ermine.

Chapter 13

HELL AND DAMNATION

The sloe eyes take a tour and when they return to mine they're wearing question marks.

'I was looking for a broom,' I mumble, 'to clean up the glass.'

'Really. Well, you're not going to find one there.' The voice is as dry as desiccated coconut. 'I keep my brooms in the broom cupboard.'

The breeze through the broken window tries to ruffle the dame's hair as she seats herself next to the table with the bottle on it, but her hair's too wet to be ruffled. She's changed into a nice dress under the coat and she's well into her third whisky.

'I wonder who the gunman was?' She stares at me wide-eyed. 'And I also wonder why you searched my house.'

'I had to make sure you were safe.'

'Which, of course, can be taken two ways …'

'Most things can.'

She grimaces into her whisky.

'Must you be such a tough guy?'

'Does anyone have to be anything?'

Damnation puts down her glass and hugs herself. She's got beautiful full lips to go with the eyes but the way the mouth's set could make it that of a teacher upset by the behaviour of a student.

'I trusted you, Mr Rain, yet you …' She clenches her fist; it's a good thing it's not holding the glass. 'But now I feel – defiled.'

'It was for your own good.'

'How could searching my house be for my own good? I didn't invite you into my life – you invited yourself. Along with some cock-and-bull story about an ex-wife stealing a child.'

'Except it's the truth. You were their teacher, remember?'

'But why come back for seconds? Why didn't you just leave me alone.'

I get to my feet.

'It looks like I better go.'

'Good. But before you do, tell me this: did you come back just to search my house?'

I decide to tell her too much. But maybe I intended doing that all along.

'No. I'm leaving the country and I wanted to see you before I went.'

The eyes soften. 'Where are you going?' She answers her own question. 'You're going to France, aren't you? I don't need to be a private inquiry agent to know that. Well, you've seen me so now you can go. *Bon chance a decouvrir ta fille.*'

I play it dumb.

'I beg your pardon?'

She smiles triumphantly.

'I said, good luck finding your daughter when you don't even speak French.'

She moves closer to me. Rube taught me to let them open the door so I step aside. But instead of opening the door the dame gazes up at me out of her sloe eyes and says, 'Mr Rain …?'

'Mr Rain what?'

'Why don't you take me with you?'

She's put a nice red-and-white check cloth on the table and there's a bottle of French wine, salt and pepper pots in the shape of overstuffed ducks, a red candle, two plates and a hot baking tray containing a margherita pizza with too many olives in it.

'I could be useful,' she says. 'And you might just find yourself in need of *useful*.' She leans forward. 'I mean, have you ever even *been* to France?'

'Not in so many words.'

'And you don't speak French.'

Sometimes ignorance can be bliss – hers if not mine.

'Again, not in so many words.'

She sits back. 'So in so many words you'd be *fou* if you *didn't* take me.'

I know the question's brutal but it's the brutal questions you got to ask in this world. Life's a series of them, even when the answers turn out to be ones you don't want to hear.

'What's in it for you? Dames don't just fly off to

foreign countries with strangers, even when those countries aren't all that foreign to them.'

Damnation silently plays with her fork like she's trying to splay the prongs.

'Maybe you feel homesick,' I continue. 'But that's not enough.' I wave a hand at our surrounds. 'You live in a big house. You got a rich lover. Yet you're prepared to toss it away for a trip to France with a stranger. It's what people do when they're teenagers. And it doesn't add up to a row of peanuts when they're not.'

In the dim light of the candle on the red-and-white tablecloth, her amethyst eyes go opaline.

'I – I –'

She's been shot at, which gives her an idea of what could happen if she hooks up with me. And she's had her house strip-searched, which ditto. I'm a lunk with a gun and about as much class as a corpse in a sewer.

'Just answer the question.'

She wipes her eyes on a corner of the tablecloth and takes a deep breath.

'Maybe if I told you something about myself …'

Chapter 14

THE PROFILE CHANGER

Hélène Dalmation was born in Toulouse, France – about a decade after my mother produced me in a dam in Nimbin, Australia – the result of a union between a Parisian seamstress and a Basque terrorist.

'A what?'

She tucks an errant lock behind a beautiful ear. Thanks to the breeze, her hair's drying nicely and after she tucks back the curl, the shine in the eyes seems no longer due to the tears. 'Oh, Basque terrorists are nothing like – well, people who fly planes into buildings,' she explains. 'In fact, they personify the ideals most French like to imagine they possess, courtesy of the Revolution – liberty, equality and fraternity. The belief that all people are equal and no-one's any better than anyone else.'

When her father was killed, her mother couldn't cope so baby Hélène was sent to a nunnery. At sixteen, she escaped, marrying the scion of a wealthy Australian family, who was in France doing nothing in preparation for doing nothing for the rest of his life. The happy couple drifted to Australia, and after the divorce Damnation discovered herself in the withered but welcoming arms of Albert Flax.

She spreads her hands and the shadows of her fingers play Ludo on the tablecloth.

'Which brings us to now.'

'Tell me about Flax.'

'What's to tell? He's an ex-Olympian, he's rich and he's very generous.'

'And you love him?'

She shrugs. 'What's not to love?'

'Yet you're prepared to ditch him for a trip to France with someone you just met?'

She considers me over the hands.

'Your ex-wife ditched you for as little.' She picks up the pepper pot and puts it down again, raising her eyes to mine. 'I can go back to France whenever I want. Albert isn't possessive.' She takes another deep breath. 'But being *able to* isn't the same as *wanting to*. And the reason I want to go to France is because, well, I – I like you.'

She's young and she's beautiful but I've still got half a brain to think with.

'You're being impulsive. From what you told me, you're in the habit of doing things you later regret. You want to go to France with me just like you came to Australia with Mr Useless and later fetched up with Mr ex-Olympian.'

'It's not like that.'

I ask the question and I ask it sudden.

'What about Mr Green?'

'I've already told you –' she fiddles with the candle '– I don't even *know* your Mr Green. He was never more than a – a silhouette in a car to me.' When she reaches across the remains of the pizza, the hand on mine is warm. It must be because of the candle.

'But I can help you find him if I accompany you to France.'

I tell her *okay*.

I'm only human.

Apart from which, having her along might help me to find Imogene.

Rube's detached herself from Mr Heartbreak for the afternoon and she's clutching a book and kneeling by two suitcases – one big and one small – in the aft companionway of the *Wooden No*. She looks better but looks can be illusory.

'This book's called *France at a Glance* and you'll need to read it during the plane ride, so it goes in the cabin bag. In the big wheelie bag I've packed nice, warm flannelette pyjamas, several pairs of socks, a toothbrush – and an electric razor. And here's the passport.'

The boat lurches as Rube flips open the little black book with the bird and marsupial on the front. I feel dizzy. It's strange existing, even if it's only temporarily and in the guise of someone else. Or maybe it's just the boat lurching.

'Arthur Halliwell,' Rube reads aloud. She looks up, comparing my face with the photograph. 'Not a bad likeness – except for the baldness. Who was he?'

I tell her what Ace wrote in the note accompanying the passport that found its way into Ruby's letterbox. Halliwell was a case of mistaken identity resulting in accidental death, courtesy of an Australian

Federal Police hit squad. Too late, they discovered that Halliwell wasn't a terrorist at all, just a meek and mild suburban accountant who keyed *bomb* into his computer one day when he meant *porn*. No history, no family, few friends, so the death went unreported. Similar features to mine, except for the baldness.

Rube nods.

'I've also packed some nice grey suits, a grey cardigan and a grey Akubra. You won't know yourself.'

She shifts on her knees – the tube writhing under her jacket – and produces the kind of wallet an accountant called Halliwell might carry.

'Inside you'll find something to help with expenses.' I start to protest. 'Don't argue with me, Rainbow – think of it as an early inheritance. God knows, with my kidney the way it is there's unlikely to be a late one.'

'You're a long way from dying, Rube.'

'I'm not talking about me dying, I'm talking about you living.'

She shuts the suitcase as the boat yaws and the pump makes obscene noises in the bilge. Then she clambers to her feet.

'That closes that case. Now all you need concern yourself with is the one concerning the kid.' She glances over the railing like she's surprised to find we're still afloat. 'And don't worry, I'll look after the *Wooden No* while you're away.'

'And who's going to look after you?'

Rube grabs hold of a stanchion as a wave rocks us.

'Rory's offered. There's no need to grimace, he

might be Rory, but he's – whatever he is. So keep your hair on.' She shoots me a wan smile. 'Or off, as the case may be.'

'Did your tame spook provide you with anything else?' Rube asks as my locks scatter.

I nod and the blades nick my right lug – the one Madam Lash missed in the *Horses for Corpses* caper. I feel the wind lick at the cut.

'Yeah, he came up with an itinerary. As for Lifar, he flew out yesterday on a Boeing 747 bound for Heathrow, London – business class.'

'Is that his final destination?'

'Ace thinks he's headed for France. Which makes it a match.'

'How do you know that's where Salina and the kid are?'

'Because Ace says so.'

Rube ditches the shears and switches to the buzz cut. 'Good old Ace,' she murmurs. 'But Lifar needed Salina and Imogene to fuzz-up his image. So their travelling separately suggests two things:

'There was no *physical* coercion on Salina and the kid to accompany him; and

'Lifar's nothing but a dumbstruck lover, after all.'

I cop another pinch, this time to the other ear, and this time from the buzzer.

'Maybe he just wanted to look different *after* he arrived,' I suggest. 'Remember, they're probably not expecting me to come after them.'

Rube nods and I duck, thereby avoiding further bloodshed. For the moment.

'Assuming they meet up in Paris, where will they go after that?' she asks.

'I'll have to work that out when I get there. With a bit of luck I can grab the kid and bring her home. Like I said, Salina won't be expecting me. She can follow me and Imogene back or stay where she is with Lifar.'

Despite my display of assurance, Rube looks worried.

'That ignores the attack on me and the bullets, Rainbow. I got mugged, remember? And a dancer got *killed*. What if this is more than just a simple abduction?'

I touch my integument and cartilage and my hand comes away spotted with blood.

'We play it by ear – if I've still got any left after you're done with them.'

But Rube's not interested in herrings, red or otherwise.

'You said *we*.' She waves her instrument of torture at the Harbour. 'Who's *we*?'

As an interrogator, Rube's got no equal. Torquemada would have had to wait in line if Rube was around during the Spanish Inquisition.

'You needn't come the detective with me, Rube, I –'

Her mouth tightens. '*Who's* going with you, Rainbow?'

I take a deep breath. It's got hairs in it but no graces.

'Yeah, well, there's this dame called Hell and Damnation, see, and …'

'Hell and *who*?'

The ship rolls and I roll with it.

'Yeah, well …' Rube calls it my *yeah-and-welling* – when she hears me *yeah-and-welling* she knows that I'm stalling. 'It's pronounced *Hay-leng Dah-mah-shong* but I call her Damnation. She's the dame who taught Salina and the kid French and has been helping me with my inquiries. She'll change my profile.'

Rube examines her cutters.

'Just like Delilah did with Samson. Won't you ever learn? This Damnation's danger. The name's enough. You're not on some *jaunt*, you know. You're trying to find your kid.'

'She could have a tie-in with Lifar, Rube. And she speaks French. Plus she was at the ballet when the dancer was shot.' I don't quit while I'm ahead. 'Also I want her where I can put my hands on her.'

Rube's mouth forms a thin line, like she's in a great deal of pain and I've just added to it.

'You know how to speak French, Rainbow, remember?'

'Yeah, but she speaks it better.'

'I think you just want this dame where you can put your hands on her.'

I feel my eyes snow over and my worldview grow less bleak. 'Yeah, there's that, too.'

Chapter 15

PAY ATTENTION TO
THE FOLLOWING

You become what you're wearing. And I'm wearing undertaker's smart-casual – grey daks, wide-lapelled jacket featuring too many brass buttons, shoestring tie, shiny black slime-ons – plus a grey Akubra with a brim so wide it could double as an umbrella. All of which turns me into an unassuming suburban accountant called Arthur Halliwell.

That, plus a suitcase full of the kind of possessions an unassuming suburban accountant might take with him to a double-entry bookkeeping convention in Paris, if he hadn't been occupying a plot in Rookwood cemetery. Which is what he's doing and how come I'm wearing his passport. Garbed in the unfamiliar clobber and possessed of an identity, I feel myself change – not just in appearance but in the way I think and the way I speak. Rube warned me it could happen. Me and the dame are on stand-by and I got Rube's tour book open at the section called 'Handy Travel Tips', which begins:

'You'll keep coming across familiar faces. But don't worry, it doesn't mean you're being followed ...'

The dame left me minding her bags while she went

to the Ladies and now she's craning her beautiful neck checking the flight board for the plane we couldn't get seats on. She's dressed in what she calls the year-before-last Parisian chic – red silk scarf, cerise suit that highlights the colour of her eyes, and stockings you can hardly see at all, that really suit her legs.

Perched beside her is her wheelie case with the purple flowers on the outside and too many toiletries on the inside. I know because I checked while she was in the Ladies. The dame's clean. Or at least her suitcase is. I go back to the advice in the travel book:

'... *It's just folk on much the same journey of discovery you're on.*'

'You're in luck, there have been two cancellations and the seats happen to be next to each other.' The woman at the check-in counter glances from me to Damnation and back again. 'Passports, please, and place your bags on the conveyor belt.'

We hand her our passports – one black, the other red.

'Mr Halliwell and Ms Dalmation.' The woman does her check. 'Father and daughter?'

'Just good friends,' I say, glancing behind us in case someone's listening.

'Are you all right, Rainbow?'

I frown Damnation into silence. 'You must be thinking of someone else,' I mutter. 'The name's Arthur Halliwell. In fact, anything other than the name you just said.'

Damnation colours. She looks nice, coloured. She looks nice in black and white, too.

'I'm sorry,' she whispers. 'But give me a break, Rai – I mean, Arthur. I'm still getting used to the baldness.'

The woman at the check-in counter smiles like she's thinking about anything else as she hands back our passports, plus two bits of cardboard that make us temporary owners of a pair of adjoining seats on a plane to Paris.

'Please go straight to the departure gate or you'll miss your flight. And that would be sad after waiting all this time for a cancellation, wouldn't it?' The check-in woman glances behind us. 'Ah, some late arrivals.'

An elderly couple step into our vacuum, smiling apologetically. Behind them is a man in black – wearing a hard bag and an even harder look – and I got to restrain Damnation because it's not smart to run at airports. Run and you draw attention to yourself. Run and you'll be dragged kicking and screaming to the interrogation room. Run and you'll be on their files forever, listed as people who are in the habit of running at airports.

When we reach customs and immigration, I take off my Akubra for a person in uniform, who asks, 'Business or pleasure?'

I reply that we're going to *Romantasy-land* at which the official smiles because officialdom's just like Salina and a lot more romantic than people think. He stamps our passports and we proceed along to baggage check, where I place my sober braces and sober shoes and even more sober hat in the plastic tray provided and hold up my hands so they can see if I wash under my armpits. And all the time I'm watching for anyone that might be becoming too familiar like:

The elderly couple behind us; and

The man in black.

Damnation touches my arm.

'We're through.' I give her the eyebrow-raise. 'I mean through the last barrier – not as a couple. We're almost on the plane. It's like we're entering a new world.'

I shake my Yul Brynner skull at her.

'There's no such thing as a new world, only more of the old. But if it helps to keep the fire alive, I'll come along for the bride.'

We've scored an aisle and an inner – the kind you've got to climb over everyone else just to get to the toilet. The man in black's in the seat behind me, taking up too much overhead luggage space with his oversized cabin bag.

Time for a position statement:

My ex has taken the kid;

They're in Paris; and

I don't know if I can trust the dame but it sure is nice she's here.

Chapter 16

CHARACTERS ON A PLANE

We stay on the plane for the Singapore refuel. The dame's got a nice line in patter. In fact, she's got a nice line, period. Also, she sleeps a fair bit, which allows me to do my homework. I've got no idea what Salina's up to, except more of the same. And I don't know what's happened to Imogene. Is Mr Green – alias Lifar – just an innocent lover? And how the hell do I find out? I've got half an idea, but sometimes half an idea's worse than no idea at all. I half-watch a movie about identity theft while reconstructing the evidence.

Salina ran off with Lover Boy and took the kid along for the ride. But if Salina wanted to be in the City of Love with her boyfriend, wouldn't it have been smarter to leave Immo behind? The kid was prevented from leaving a forwarding address, managing no more than one tape-recorded word and a cancelled ticket to the ballet. Which means that, after all the French lessons, it was a plain and simple abduction. But why would Salina abduct her own daughter? To get back at me? If so, why was Rube mugged? And what about the death of the ballet dancer?

I drag my eyes away from the movie and find myself staring at the safety pamphlet in the seat pocket in front of me. It's printed on nice, glossy paper – just like the stuff in the rats' nest behind the water heater at Salina's joint.

When Rube did jigsaws, she used to put the bits on a board so they wouldn't fly around. I retrieve the evidence bag from my pocket and set out the rat-chewed scraps on the safety pamphlet. People see what they want to see. That means the pieces will fall where I *expect* them to fall instead of where they belong. Beside me Damnation shifts in her sleep, bumping my elbow and knocking the letters out of position. A voice over the PA says, 'We are experiencing flatulence. Please return to your seats and fasten your seatbelts.'

Only it's not *flatulence* but *turbulence*. Spelled: *T-U-R-B-U-L-E-N-C-E*. I do what the voice says and the letters shift some more. *For God's sake, Rainbow,* Rube would say, *you're seeing what you* think *you see. Look at what's there, not some pie in the sky.* I steady myself. The word might be *GRENE* instead of *GREEN*. Or it could be …

The plane lurches and the dame jerks upright.

'Wha –?'

A stewardess hurrying down the aisle leans down.

'It's all right,' she tells the dame. 'Have a great trip. Enjoy.'

A great trip. Enjoy. G-R-E-A-T-T-R-I-P-E-N-J-O-Y. That includes *TRIPE* and *JOY*. Take away *ATTRIP* and *JOY* and what's left? *G-R-E-E-N*. I'm like a blind man suddenly able to see. Because I'm not supposed to be looking at the letters I've got, but for the letters that are missing. *Green*'s a red herring. Instead it's –

'What is it, Rai – Arthur?'

The main cabin lights have been switched off and my dinky little personal light is all that's illuminating the letters. Damnation wouldn't have seen anything.

'Go back to sleep,' I say. 'It's nothing – just some characters on a plane.'

I look down again and see what I've always seen – the word *Green*. But superimposed on that is the face of my daughter. The letters were in what the hostess said – *GREeat trip ENjoy*. But what I've got is different because the missing letters are different. It's *GRE*-something-*E*-something-*N* and maybe something else. The turbulence eases. I re-bag the scraps, pocket the bag, tilt back my chair, close my eyes … and don't go to sleep.

Because someone's tapping my shoulder. I resist the normal reaction. Instead I turn nice and slow to find the man in the seat behind staring at me out of hard eyes.

'You just tipped back your seat, fella,' he says. 'And you made me spill my Fanta. You might have warned me.'

A scar bisects one eyebrow, giving his eyes a cross-legged look, his mouth's fighting a losing battle with a sneer, and his hands are knotting for a fight. Or maybe he just wants attention.

'Yeah,' I reply. 'Then again I mightn't have.'

He half-stands but a stewardess closes in and he sits.

'Next time,' he mutters.

'If you're not careful, pal,' I mutter back, 'there won't be a next time.'

While other kids were told stories from Dr Seuss, Roald Dahl and Hans Christian Andersen, Aunt Rube dissected cases of the Yank detectives called the Pinkertons, whose motto under an unblinking eye was: WE NEVER SLEEP.

The man in black's behind me.

I make like the Pinkertons and keep my eyes open.

Chapter 17

ON DEATH RUE

Horns blare and drivers scream, even though the WALK sign's the same colour as the park. It's springtime in Paris and Damnation's clutching my hand. She's got a stranglehold on my heart, too. We're in the colonnade next to the Rue de Rivoli – the boulevard beside the Louvre – and the traffic's exhibiting all the enthusiasm of a scorpion, just before his girlfriend eats him.

I'm keeping a close eye on the man in black who's been on the shadow since we left Charles de Gaulle aerodrome. He was behind us during the changeover from the aboveground train to the Metro then he turned up in our carriage where he pretended interest in everything but us.

After that, he took the same wrong turns we took, ending up behind us at Gare d'Orsay. He's mingling with the pimps, hip-swingers and deros like he belongs here, ambling when we amble, stopping when we stop, feigning interest in something – anything – whenever I look his way. He's just stopped and put his bag down on the footpath beside him and he's simulating interest in a bad copy of Rodin's statue *The Thinker*.

'Come on,' I tell the dame. 'We got a job to do.'

Damnation's reluctant.

'I know,' she replies, 'but ...'

'Listen to me: we're being followed so I want you to pretend we're lovers, okay? Be careful you don't dislodge the hat and whatever you do, don't look behind you.'

Damnation's sloe eyes shift like she's about to do what I just told her not to so I pull her to me and give her a smooch, the way lovers are supposed to in Paris, without taking my eyes off the man in black. Damnation turns co-operative, but she's also trying to turn around. 'Don't look surprised and don't look behind you,' I repeat. 'I'm going to let go. When I do, we're going to split up and I'll meet you in fifteen minutes at the first café on the Rue Saint-Denis.' The last I see of Damnation is a flash of red scarf swinging around the corner, our cabin bags under her arms and our wheelie cases trundling behind her.

The instant she's gone I hurl myself back onto the street of death they call the Rue de Rivoli. As I dive, I pull my hat down over my baldness.

Sometimes tails hesitate and sometimes they don't. This one doesn't. Without looking either to his left or his right like he should have, the man in black comes after me. I leap over a Smart car and land in an arabesque. From behind – above the roar of the traffic – I hear the yell of an onlooker that tells me I'm still being followed. I face the traffic. Holding onto my hat, I do a tumble-turn over the slippy-slide bonnet of a Citroën. From behind comes the screech of brakes and a series of sickening thuds.

I turn to find the road a mess of multi-coloured metal and people gesticulating. The Rue de Rivoli will never be the same again. Neither will the man in black. He's been hit by a car, thrown across the street and is now lying crumpled in a heap in the gutter.

Within seconds, sirens sound, but something tells me I should stick around. The cops arrive and one bends over the body in the gutter and lifts it up, checking for vital signs. But then he goes one step further. He reaches into the man's pocket, retrieving something that glints in the warm Parisian sunlight.

Chapter 18

THE CLAWED HAND

Following a serious traffic incident, the cops should be stringing out the coloured tape. But they aren't. They should be measuring skid marks. But they aren't. And they should be recording witness statements. Except they aren't doing that either.

Instead, they're handing out what look like business cards to the drivers involved in the pile-up and anyone else that happens to be passing. Keeping the brim of my accountant's Akubra well down I head back into the action. The fuzz in France are divided into local, state and what's known as the Sûreté Nationale. The Sûreté are the big boys and they're the ones handing out the cards. Traffic accidents don't usually involve them. A tow truck appears, along with Parisian street cleaners. A cop approaches. I clutch my chest with one hand, hold out my free mitt and receive a card.

After that I cross the road and head north, rough-translating as I go: *All this will be sorted. You do not need to contact an insurance agent. Nor do you need a lawyer. Your damages will be attended to. You will not be out of pocket. Just call the number below.*

When I reach the other side, I look to see what

the cops are doing with the body. They're handling it – if not by the book or with kid gloves – at least carefully. But no-one's noticed the bag: it's still sitting where the man in black dumped it. I pick it up like it belongs to me, check the street cameras, get out of their range, bend and unzip the bag. Dirty clothes: scrunched-up shirts, ragged singlets, crumpled underpants, crushed daks. The man in black's bag's been through airport security so there's not going to be anything insecure in it. But there's nothing of anything in it. No books, no papers, no shaver, not even a toothbrush. I rezip it and replace it where he dumped it while he was pretending too much interest in a bad copy of Rodin's *The Thinker*. Before he stopped thinking and leapt to his death.

Damnation's sitting on a cane chair at a cane table with a glass top outside the café on the Rue Saint-Denis, her mobile on the table before her and our cases on the footpath beside her. When she sees me she looks concerned. I'm carrying a fresh bruise or two and my clothes could be cleaner. Or maybe she's worried about something completely different.

'What happened?' she asks.

'Someone had a little accident. Must have been the food.'

She takes a deep breath. It reminds me of something. It reminds her of something else.

'Do you know Les Halles, the shopping mall?' she asks. 'I need to buy some summer clothes.'

But I've got other things on my mind besides fashion. I help myself to her phone.

'Before we do anything I got to make a call. And after I've done that, we got to find the flat.'

'I was just –'

I know what she was 'just', but I still check her call log, particularly the activity since we split up, after which I enter the number on the card. It's answered immediately and I'm put through to Special Branch, that section of the French police dealing with unusual cases, so I sever the connection and hand back the phone. I flip the garçon couple of Euros, grab the wheelie bags and head down the rue. Damnation's stilettos play Bach's fugue in C-minor on the footpath behind me. Behind that again is the echo of the body of the man in black being hit by a car. I don't look back.

Seine is the name of the famous Parisian waterway. It's also the English word for a dragnet to catch fish in. But I'm a long way from catching anything as we reach the address Ace gave me – a Haussmann seven-floorer, if you count the bit they put in for the birds in the roofline just above the eaves. On the footpath outside, a Parisian beggar, almost totally hidden under a grey blanket, is sitting with an upturned cap beside him.

A pair of big doors – a doghole in one of them for when the doors are locked – open onto a courtyard. Inside, there are a lot of flagstones and too many doors leading off the flagstones. A dinky little button next to a doorway says: *Artemis Bonnet, Concierge, Pressez.* I *pressez.*

An elderly dame opens the door, bending to restrain the one-eyed goat beside her. The dame's got pink-tinted hair, rose-coloured glasses, a face like a gargoyle off the nearby Notre Dame cathedral and a mouth like she's had a bad day at the dentist's. The goat tilts its head because of the eye.

'Waddayawan?' she asks in French.

'Say what we want,' I murmur to Damnation.

Damnation tells the landlady what we want.

Forget Paris chic. The space above the eaves meant for the pigeons is rubbish and we're stuck with it for a week because that's how they let these joints. Except we won't be here any longer than it takes to work out where Salina, Imogene and Lover Boy have gone. Damnation looks about her.

'The concierge said this was where they stayed,' she tells me, like telling me might take her mind off the poky surrounds. 'There was a man, a woman who was headstrong and a girl. The concierge said the girl was cute.'

All of which I know already because I speak French. Only I don't tell Damnation that. I also know the landlady gave us a funny look when she handed us the keys. But maybe that's how she always looks.

'Well, the apartment's – different, anyway.'.

'You wanted romantic.'

'Yes, but *this* romantic?'

There's a hallway, a living room, a kitchen, two bedrooms and a bathroom with a shower. A few downlights dot the tatty ceilings, seashell wallpaper decorates the walls and there are a couple of pieces of cardboard furniture. Also there's a window. The place is spotless. Just like Salina's.

'It could be the wrong apartment,' the dame says.

I shake my head. 'No, it's the right one, all right.' I've got myself up and onto the kitchen sink where I'm probing the gap between cupboards and wall with a coathanger I found in one of the cardboard wardrobes.

The dame's wearing her year-before-last clobber and shifting from one foot to the other in the doorway to the hall. 'So can I go shopping now?'

Chapter 19

SPRING SACRIFICE

A lot of stairways in Paris are corkscrew affairs and the one in our apartment block's no exception, its oak treads worn low by two centuries of sole-searching all the way to the ground floor, its balustrades as graceful as Marie Antoinette before she found herself at the wrong end of a guillotine.

As well as the corkscrew stairs there's a lift. Damnation takes the lift and I give her thirty seconds then take the stairs slow and soft while all the time listening to the lift. The lift doors open and the dame's footsteps emerge. I allow her time to reach the street, after which I step out into the courtyard. I feel eyes on me. It's the landlady, Artemis, craning to see as she bends to restrain the goat. I tip my hat. She doesn't acknowledge the gesture. Beside her the goat closes its one good eye and stares at me blindly out of the other.

I exit via the little dog-door, pass the beggar on the footpath, and head after Damnation.

Les Halles is in the opposite direction to the one she's taken.

Question 1: Why did she lie to me?

Question 2: Where is she really going?

Question 3: What else has she lied to me about?

There are more curves to this dame than there are in a Parisian staircase. But it makes her easy to tail.

All I got to do is follow the stares.

Because of the Revolution there's nothing left of the jail they called the Bastille. But as Damnation passes what's not left of the jail, I can still hear the clatter of the guillotine and smell the blood … before realising it's only the modern-day French enjoying the fruits of the Revolution – freedom and the demise of the hated aristocrats.

Meanwhile the stares tell me the dame's chucked a left followed by a right. In my suit I follow suit. She's not looking behind her, which means she's not aware I'm following her. Or else she's very aware and pretending she's not. I stay well back in case of either.

There's a lot of expensive shops in Paris but Le Printemps is the biggie, stretching over several blocks and selling perfumes, fashion and bric-a-brac that normal money can't buy. As I enter, a dame in a black frock disinfects me with gold-plated aftershave. Silver gee-gaws disguised as lobsters are a pinch at ten grand a claw. Tourists shove one another out of the way to get at the bargains. I keep my eye on the dame as she weaves her way towards the –

My legs suddenly go weak. In Le Printemps – which means *spring* – the French imagination has gone into overdrive. Over the PA they're playing none other than the Stravinsky ballet *The Rite of Spring* in the belief that most people won't make the connection. *The Rite of Spring* is about sacrifice and I no longer see shoppers but the heads, arms and outstretched hands of executioners –

Meanwhile I've lost sight of Damnation. There are no longer any people staring and telling me where she went because everyone's too busy shopping. I'm stuck in a Parisian orgy, a Bacchanalia, a Saturnalia, and the music's giving me the heebies. I got to escape, out of this bloody music of sacrifice, away from the memory of what was and the dread of what might be.

I stumble from the store but the music follows me, music depicting innocence in the face of evil – a child faced by impending death – and in my mind I see Pandora. As I reach the footpath outside, the music reaches a crescendo. The racket of the traffic hits me but compared to what I'm trying to escape, it's breath after asphyxiation, light after dark, life after death.

I hurtle back to the apartment on the Rue de Rivoli.

Chapter 20

WHAT THE CONCIERGE SAW

The sun's still shining and the beggar outside the apartment block's still begging, an indeterminate shape beneath a blanket. While in the courtyard, the landlady's watering her pansies in the company of her goat.

'*Tout va bien?*' she says.

She's asking how I am but I'm not supposed to know what she's saying.

'Sorry but I don't speak French.'

She does a sideways tilt of her head, much like the goat, and her eyes grow cunning.

'Oh, really?' she replies in English.

'Yeah, really.'

The goat stamps a curled-over hoof and lowers its horned head while the old woman looks like she's heard it all before and returns to her watering.

'Things can die from too much attention, Artemis,' I tell her.

She doesn't look up.

'Fifty euro.'

'I already paid the rent.'

She crosses to a tap shaped like a gargoyle to refill her watering can. All I can see is her hunched back and the bearded profile of the goat. I've got to strain to hear what she says over the noise of the traffic.

'I'm not talking about the rent.' She turns off the gargoyle, crosses to a cactus and continues negotiating. 'I'm a landlady in Paris. More precisely, I'm the ill-paid slave of the rich person who owns this place. Which means that, while I'm happy to pretend I'm stupid, me and Maria here still need to keep up with the cost of living. A hundred.'

'You just said fifty.'

'The cost of living just doubled.'

At the current exchange rate, a hundred euros is about a hundred and fifty Australian. I hand over the money while I can still afford it and it disappears down the landlady's cleavage like a rat down a rope. 'The woman and the girl arrived first,' she says with a crooked smile. 'The woman's French was basic but I let her struggle, pretending I didn't know English in the same way some people pretend not to know French.'

A truck rumbles past and I let the comment pass along with it.

'Your ex-wife thought she was in love. She was also clearly anxious about the girl.' The woman anticipates my next question. 'The girl didn't seem happy. I heard her say she wanted to contact her father.'

Imogene said that so the woman would hear her and pass on the information.

'What else did she say?'

Again the sly look. 'Nothing.'

'When did the boyfriend arrive?'

'A couple of days after the mother and daughter.'

The greedy look makes a return visit. She thought she'd fired all her bullets only to discover she's still got another slug in the chamber. The goat nuzzles her affectionately. Or maybe it's just scratching itself.

I palm her another fifty euros and it follows the rest down the rope.

'He couldn't keep his hands off her.'

'Were the hands caressing or restraining?'

The greedy look's replaced by a knowing one.

'In Paris, caressing and restraining mean pretty much the same thing.' I make like I want my money back. 'All right, the hands were strong.'

'That all I get for the extra fifty – that the boyfriend had strong paws?'

'I could invent things but you'd only find out.'

'What makes you say that?'

'Because you're not just a concerned father, you're also a private detective.'

'What about his face?'

'Like you, he was wearing a hat. So, like yours, his face wasn't there to describe.'

'What names did they put in your book? We wrote our names in a book so they must have, too.' She goes back into a room with a threadbare carpet lit by a barley-twist lamp, leaving the goat staring at me out of its one eye, and when she returns into the spring sunshine she's carrying a book with marbling on the outside and scribble on the inside. And what the scribble says is that one *John Smith*, in company with his wife *Ann* and daughter *Annette*, stayed in the selfsame flat we're in.

'No passport details.' I look up; the landlady's breath smells of garlic, or maybe it's the goat's.

'Don't you have to see passports?'

She shakes her head.

'The man paid extra not to show their passports.'

'How long did they stay?'

'He was in a hurry. Two days, but they paid for a week.'

'Did he possess any distinguishing characteristics?'

'His hands were beautiful.'

'Anything else?'

Then – but only after looking down at the goat, apparently considering whether she should do an Oliver Twist and ask for more – she replies, 'Yes, there was something else.'

'What?'

'The Monsieur was very interested in the beggar in the Rue de Rivoli.'

Chapter 21

NO VISIBLE MEANS OF SUPPORT

I'm about to ask Artemis to explain when – above the racket of the traffic and the sandpaper rasp of her hand on the even rougher horns of the goat – I hear the *tap-tap-tap* of expensive new heels on the pavement. I quickly palm the dame some more euros.

'This conversation never happened,' I say.

'Do I look stupid?'

I'm in the scullery when Damnation returns hugging enough parcels to send Santa Claus into early retirement. She looks far too innocent to be anything but guilty.

'How was Les Halles?' I ask.

'I didn't go to Les Halles. It's being rebuilt. I went to Le Printemps instead, the store that's *not* Galeries Lafayette ...'

I know Galeries Lafayette. I also know the dame's telling the truth. I came back via Les Halles and all

I saw for my trouble was a whole lot of hoardings. Damnation glances around the flat before looking back at me and when she does her eyes widen.

'Have you been here all this time?'

'What did you buy?'

She shakes her parcels. 'Would you like a parade?'

I'd like a parade like I'd like a hole in the head that's not my nose, ears or eyes, but I tell her, *Yeah, I'll go with the show*. After she disappears into her room, I cross to the window overlooking the Rue de Rivoli. The beggar below is hidden by the sort of blanket Napoleon's soldiers might have worn on the retreat from Moscow – full of hard luck stories and holes and covered with stains that might be blood. No shape you could call a shape, its head tucked away like a cockatoo's on a bad night in Innamincka. The torso's parallel to the pavement and it's got no visible means of support.

'Why are you looking out the window when you should be looking at me?'

If I thought the dame was beautiful before, I was wrong. *This* is beautiful. She's dragged her hair back into a chignon to reveal her full magnificence – the sloe eyes, retroussé nose, soft mouth set in a half-smile, a neck that would be at home on a swan, and a body that might as well be naked. The dress is all but transparent, showing that – just like the beggar on the street outside – Damnation's got no visible means of support.

'Well, what do you think?' she asks.

I don't tell her what I think. Tell her what I think and the temple would collapse. I force myself to remember she's nothing more than a translator on legs and a profile changer. As well as possibly completely untrustworthy. So instead of telling her what I think, I ask, 'What did it cost?'

Her shoulders sag. 'Is that all you can say?' She glares at me but after a while she stops glaring. 'Oh well, I'll take it as an attempt at a compliment and show you more.'

While the dame takes a shower after the show – this time I don't ask where she's taking it – I return to checking out the beggar. There's something about his shape that's not quite right. It could be female but it's so far removed from the one under the shower, it could be an orangutan. I grab my hat.

'I'm going out!' I shout.

The steam coming from beneath the bathroom door has just reminded me of the smoke in the *Rite of Spring*, if I needed reminding. *The Monsieur was very interested in the beggar in the Rue de Rivoli*, the landlady said.

There aren't any clues in the flat as to where Salina and Imogene might be.

That just leaves the beggar in the Rue de Rivoli.

Chapter 22

THE BEGGAR IN THE RUE DE RIVOLI

I don't look his way as I climb through the dog-door. Instead I stare at the Parisian skyline like I'm surprised to find it's still there. After which I turn and head east, taking a line parallel with the river. A block later I find a tabac which has got a seat by the window with a view to the beggar.

One of Rube's lessons: *The French are a naked tribe, their country exposed on all sides to their enemies. When people are exposed, they don armour. Or they wear attitude like it's chainmail. What's Latin for warm? Calere, I'd reply. Turn it into the negative. Noncalere. Now for the tot of rum, what is it in French? Non chalere? Close but no Bundy. It's nonchaloir. Which means non-heat, indifference, cool. And in English that becomes? Nonchalant.* And that's what the clientele is when I enter the tabac: they pretend I don't exist. Which is fine by me because it's my natural state. It also leaves me free to examine the beggar up the road. Passers-by drop coins in the cap and the figure under the blanket doesn't thank the donors, doesn't even move.

Until, thirty-seven minutes into the surveill, a

claw darts out to retrieve something dropped by a stroller: male, slight build, mackintosh, hat pulled down over eyes. Who afterwards crouches and disappears through the dog-door into the apartment block. I can't make out what was dropped. Just that the beggar picks it up and immediately resumes its posture while the dog-door flaps shut behind the raincoat …

Like I said, a lot of detecting's waiting. I wait until my legs go numb, my head's whirling, and I'm suffering acute caffeine poisoning. An inebriate bumps against me and doesn't apologise. This is Paris. Rude's *de rigueur*. The bartender wipes something red off a glass. It might be lipstick or it might be blood. The beggar moves.

At first it's no more than a twitch, the kind of movement a snake might make at the entrance to a burrow, barely perceptible to the rabbit unless the rabbit's looking. Which most of the time it's not. Another coffee arrives and the claw appears again. I'm too far away to make out the details, only that the claw comes out and an arm follows.

The arteries of the human body are positioned on the inner thighs in order not to be exposed. But whoever came up with that little idea didn't take into account surveilling. I been sitting too long for my legs to function properly and when I get onto the footpath I stagger. The weather's turned cold or maybe it's my apprehension. I work my way through the bloodlessness in my legs, drag my hat down over my baldness and start in the direction of the beggar.

There's too much traffic – motor and pedestrian – so I stick to the gutter. On my approach, the figure straightens and shucks off the blanket, to reveal:

The secret of how it defied gravity – a steel post sticking out of the footpath; and

That it's a *he* and he's around my height – just over the six-foot-two mark – but slimmer. He'd only weigh 160 pounds – 75 kilos – but his muscles are like steel cable. Most startlingly, he's dressed neck-to-toe in skin-tight white, his head and hands painted the same colour as the garb.

His head swivels and his snake eyes fix on mine.

Chapter 23

PURSUING PROTEUS

One minute he's there, the next minute he's gone. But he was there for a reason and that reason involved Imogene. It's difficult for a big man to hide. Paint him white and it becomes impossible. But he's *protean* – as in *Proteus*, the mythological being who could assume any shape he wanted. The beggar seems to change shape and as he does so he merges. And he's wearing his hurry-shoes.

I pound along in his wake, traversing the north side of the Rue de Rivoli while heading in the direction of the Champs Elysees, chasing a too-white figure with a too-white head bobbing above the rest of the pedestrians like a big white poppy in a paddock of pansies. It's peak hour so the traffic's at a standstill. There's no chance of another accident: there's not enough circulation. Besides, Proteus is too quick as he weaves towards the Louvre.

I hold onto my hat as I struggle to keep up with my quarry. He's already in the tunnel leading to the Louvre and I'm in there after him. He sends a busker flying as he reaches the queue to the glass pyramid.

I expect him to keep on in the direction of the Tuilleries but instead he slows and swerves into the pyramid. He doesn't show a ticket. It's like he's a ghost that no-one apart from me can see. People don't paint themselves white in order not to be noticed. It's only when they're trying to hide that anyone becomes aware of them. Meanwhile I'm wearing a sober grey suit, even more sober shoes and a grey hat. That makes me Security. Under the Code Napoleon the cops can chuck you in jail, throw away the key and go home to dinner laughing. The French embrace officialdom because they're afraid of it. And as I've just become officialdom, I walk unchallenged into the Louvre.

If Paris is Paranoia Central, the Louvre is its heart and soul. Watchers watch the watchers watching the watchers and the Louvre's no exception. The trick is to become part of the system. I cup a hand to the non-existent wire in my ear and wave away the guard demanding my ticket. He gives a Gallic shrug and ushers me through.

I head in the direction taken by Proteus. He's no longer hurrying. Hurrying attracts attention. I duck under a wing of the Samothrace *Nike*, lowering my hat under the probing eyes of the cameras. Marble heads of ancient busts stare from the walls and statues stand implacable. Real people get in my way, see I'm trouble and get the hell out of it.

But Proteus has disappeared.

The Louvre's a labyrinth: big when it was built and even bigger now. Artworks, sightseers, statues and guards mingle over several levels, in several wings, in several states of contusion. A uniformed guard approaches but I cup my hand to my ear again and tell him someone's acting suspicious around the *Mona Lisa* and he hurries off to check. The cameras are tracking me so I keep my hat down and my head down under the hat. I hurry through rooms followed by more rooms, corridors followed by more corridors, artworks followed by more artworks, stairs followed by more stairs. But I know what I'm looking for.

I also know where to find it.

I've reached the Balcony of the Gods. What did Rube once say about gods? *Gods were no more than humans writ large, not the other way around as with modern-day religions. Apart from exhibiting human emotions like jealousy, hatred, lust and revenge, they also possessed human shapes.*

Around me stand life-sized statues of Diana, Bacchus, Vulcan, Neptune, Zeus, Proserpine, Cerberus guarding the gates of Hell, Echo and Narcissus, Pegasus, the Minotaur, Ariadne and Theseus, Theseus's maze, Artemis and her goat … *Think!* I tell myself. *Try and remember. What belongs where? Mount Olympus had a hierarchy and it's mirrored in the Louvre. Gods were a family and, as with most families, its members hated each other's guts.*

Diana with her bow. Hercules wrestling the serpent. Neptune rising from the waves. Poor little hobble-foot Vulcan. *All roads lead to Rome but only one leads to Imogene.* Before me stands yet another group of statues Napoleon stole on one of his campaigns. It occupies the middle ground of the balcony and they're the usual suspects – Zeus, Mars, Vulcan, Venus, Poseidon, Mithras, Diana …

A bunch of life-sized figures carved from marble – kneeling, standing, crouching, or poised to strike. While one of them … I turn away, hoping he hasn't noticed that I've seen him, fixing my gaze on the sculpted group of soldiers in the courtyard below.

He's good, I'll give him that. No, he's better than good. Street performance statues can hold their poses through thick and thicker, unmoved by kids kicking their knees and dogs peeing on their ankles, staying as still as crocodiles in a Northern Territory creek bed until …

By now, Damnation will have finished her shower and be garbing herself in her newly-acquired finery while wondering what's become of her private defective. I don't know who she is or what her game is or how she can help me find Imogene, only that she's …

Right at that very moment, Proteus makes his move.

Chapter 24

DEATH COMES TO
THE LOUVRE

I'm trapped, my back to the balcony railing, while below me the jagged points of the spears of the soldier-statues are rearing upwards. I got distracted by thoughts of the dame. Rube warned she'd be trouble. You can't be distracted in this game. Proteus has got the drop on me and he's poised for the kill, snake eyes sharp as the tips of the spears in the courtyard. That's when the Fates step in, taking the form of a tall, stooped figure in a green-brown suit that might have been woven out of moss, and a small woman in tweed. They look like they'd be more comfortable in rocking chairs on a verandah in Matraville than wandering around the Louvre. They also look familiar.

It's like the Louvre goes into freeze frame, like the statues become the sightseers and the tourists become the tableau. Time stands still. So does Proteus, as the geezer in the moss-brown suit steps forward, peering up. The slightest of tremors runs through the statue as Proteus steadies himself.

'Please, Harold!'

The woman grabs the codger's arm below his

elbow. 'But it shouldn't be here, Maud. I know this piece of statuary.' The man tries to shake himself free of his wife's grasp. 'Let me go. I need to get a closer look.'

But Maud only tightens her grip, restraining Harold from doing something even more foolish than usual. 'I realise you know all there is to know about such things, Harold, but this is the Louvre and the Louvre knows even more than you do.' She glances nervously about her then even more nervously back at her husband. But Harold moves closer to the figure that shouldn't be there – the beggar that became Proteus, the cuckoo in the nest – dragging his wife behind him.

When I was a child I drew squares in the dirt with sticks, topping them off with triangles and calling them houses. That's what witnesses do – they see the cliché. *The old man lunged forward while the old woman fell in front of him, tripping over one of the statues as she tried to steady herself. The old man was one of those statue-smashers. Why else would he be waving a hammer …?* While another onlooker, equally certain, insists someone else had the hammer and was going to whack the old man with it, except the old lady stepped in to prevent it. While a third witness –

Even I can't be certain of what happened next and I'm a trained watcher. It was all too fast for anyone to be sure of anything and too fast for me to stop it.

The statue-that's-not-a-statue makes his move. The problem is the old man's in his way when he makes it, causing the statue to swear in very un-statuesque fashion as he trips over Harold with Maud clinging onto his arm. And in the absence of any means of support – visible or otherwise – the statue goes too far off the perpendicular to have any hope of ever recovering it.

The white-marble arms with the real flesh and blood in them flail as Proteus high-steps his way towards the railing separating the balcony from the courtyard below. The whole thing looks like it's been choreographed. The statue's face is contorted with rage. He raises one leg for a round-sweeping kick at my head. I switch my attempt to save the life of the statue into a sideways-roll to save myself.

My move throws him even further off balance. He looks around wildly for a handhold but there isn't one; he tries to steady himself but momentum's got a grip on him and he freewheels backwards. The back of his knees hit the parapet and he goes over, accompanied by a piercing scream. When I get to the railing, it's to see the points of the spears have got blood on them and the blood's coming out of a no-longer-white figure that was once a statue, and before that a beggar in the Rue de Rivoli, but is now dead.

Fate happens.

The tableau turns back into people and uniforms pop up out of nowhere. I hurl myself down the stairs. The wallet's a barely-perceptible lump against the man's now-dead heart. I'm gripping his neck like I'm checking the pulse as the guard arrives, hard-faced, grey-garbed and suspicious.

'Who are you?' he demands.

I wave the man's wallet like it's ID and it's mine.

'Gendarmerie, Organisation Anti-Terrorist Française and Chief Archivist,' I say. Through the museum's thick walls I hear the sirens. 'See to the body,' I order as the rest of the cohort arrives. 'And after that, see to your security – it's got gaps you could drive a bulldozer through. I will deal with it all in my report.'

The guard nods and begins doing his job, shepherding onlookers away as more people pour into the courtyard. I glance up. The elderly couple are staring down over the railing. I tuck the wallet away, jam down my hat and melt into the artwork.

Chapter 25

IN THE CAROUSEL GARDEN

I hurry along the Corridor of Angels, past Edvard Munch's masterpiece – the one with the man with the open mouth on the bridge screaming – around the Roman ruins, to the exit. I emerge from the pyramid, get around the fountain, past the mini-triumphal arch, and into the spring-green gardens next to the carousel, hard-edged as it turns slowly against the darkening sky. I take out the wallet and examine it.

No name, no brand – but I was expecting that. No money, either. I was expecting that, too. In fact, there's nothing that *should* be in it. I crouch beside a reclining bronze nude and look for anything that *shouldn't*.

But apart from a ticket to the Louvre, the wallet's empty. I rip out the lining. More nothing – no secret compartment, no microdots, no clues as to where I might find Imogene. I replace the ticket and chuck the wallet in the bin beside the nude as blue lights flicker on the archway, heralding nightfall.

To the west stand the golden statues of the Place de la Concorde, to the south is the Seine, and to the north the slow-turning carousel. But the east is where the action is. They've put up a police barrier, the queue's dispersing and 'closed' signs hang on the doors of the pyramid. Among the tourists around the fountain, I make out the figures of Harold and Maud, the elderly couple from Antiquities. And because they're sitting instead of standing, I remember where I've seen them before – behind me and Damnation at the check-in counter at Sydney Airport, and after that beside us on the plane.

You'll keep coming across familiar faces. It doesn't mean you're being followed. They're just people on the same journey ...

A father's flying a plastic clitter-clatter bird for his kids, the lights on the carousel have become a rainbow against the sky, lovers kiss, traffic hums and a barge's tocsin sounds on the river. I put my head down as I make for the sunset, causing a little green garbage truck driven by a man in green coveralls to swerve to avoid me.

'Idiot!' shouts the driver. He shakes his head as he climbs down from the cab, crosses to a bin and empties it, still shaking his head.

I continue towards the gibbet they call la Tour Eiffel just as the sun's setting, marshalling the only facts that I'm sure of:

Salina took the kid

Rube was mugged and I don't know who did it

A dancer was murdered and ditto

I've got a few scraps of paper with letters on them that might spell GREEN

The man in black was known to the gendarmerie

The beggar in the Rue de Rivoli met with a grisly end. He didn't require a ticket to the Louvre.

Yet there was a ticket in his wallet …

I watch the little green garbage truck trundle away. Tidy lot, these Parisians. In half an hour all the bins in the Tuilleries will be empty. Tomorrow will produce more rubbish but that, too, will be swiftly dealt with. They've even got bikes with trunks on them to suck up poodle poo. They think of everything.

Just like I didn't. Because I didn't ask myself the one question I should have asked: *Why would a man who didn't need a ticket to the Louvre have a ticket to the Louvre?* The little green truck is beside the bin into which I tossed the wallet, compacting more rubbish. Gendarmes in SWAT gear are handing out cards. I break into a run.

'Hey!'

The cops look up and the cleaner straightens from replacing the insert.

'Wait!' I yell. A cop motions toward his gun. Rube on gendarmes: *French cops shoot first and ask questions later. So if you must move in the presence of the gendarmerie, move slowly. Otherwise you might never move again.* But I want to – need to – move again. So I slow to a walk and the cop lightens up. I gesture to the man in green standing beside the bin beside the statue.

'What's up?' he asks.

I indicate the truck.

'Any chance I can check your garbage?'

The man in green shakes his head.

'Ever tried opening a bottle without a corkscrew?'

It's like I just buried Imogene. Because whatever was in the wallet wasn't a ticket to the Louvre. It was what the passer-by tossed to the beggar and what the beggar picked up. The concierge told me Lifar was interested in the beggar in the Rue de Rivoli – the beggar who turned into Proteus before turning up dead. And the beggar in the Rue de Rivoli was interested in what the passer-by dropped in his cap before disappearing through the dog-door. It was my only clue. It can't have been anything else.

The cleaner's replacing the bin as I turn away. That's when I stop turning away. Because the cleaner's not replacing an empty bin but removing a full one. I spin, dive, grab the can out of his hands and empty its contents on the grass. I scrabble through the mess as the cleaner backs away. Nothing, nothing and more nothing. No wallet. No clue. No …

The cleaner opens his mouth and I expect a torrent of abuse but instead he says, 'It's not there.' He's got a little goatee, an awkward twist to the mouth behind the beard and a green canvas bag over his shoulder. I climb to my feet. He backs away, clutching the bag.

'What's not where?' I demand.

'In Paris, Monsieur, some people lose things while others find them. It's a perk of my profession – like the diamond ring a plumber comes across in a rich man's drain. One man's poison is another man's *poisson*. It's only a wallet …'

I stretch out a hand as well as the truth.

'Yeah, but it's *my* wallet.'

The street lamp's one of those wrought-iron affairs that earn Paris the title of The City of Love. A thin mist forms an oriole around the light, dimming it. But there's still enough illumination to show I'm back in the business of finding Imogene.

Because, just like I suspected, the piece of cardboard in the wallet isn't a ticket to the Louvre at all.

Chapter 26

THE RATS OF AGINCOURT

She's dead. Even in the absence of the one-eyed goat with blood in its beard I'd know, because I've been expecting it. The place is a shambles. A drinks cabinet has been upended, the barley-twist lamp's snapped in two, and while there's no light inside the unit, the curtain's torn from the window, making the street lamp outside just enough to see by. The blood's dried black and I calculate she's been dead an hour. Her torso's twisted under a reproduction Louis XIV settee while her legs form a vee that could mean victory. Except there's nothing to celebrate.

The tread of the goat's hoofs are muffled by the threadbare carpet as I pull the corpse straight.

The money I gave her in return for information is scattered over the carpet, which means robbery wasn't the motive. The killer wanted her dead and he wanted the death obvious. He wanted to stop her talking. He also wanted me – on the off-chance I survived Proteus – to know he'd stopped her, because it would warn me off.

I shove the notes into the pocket of the robe. It will help pay for the funeral. On the fridge is a magnet featuring a picture of the Arc de Triomphe and the words *I heart Paris* clamping a Post-It note to the fridge saying: *FEED THE GOAT*. I find a can labelled *For the goat* and empty its contents into a bowl. It should keep the animal away from the corpse for the night. I shut the door behind me. The lift's too slow so I take the corkscrew. But the door at the top of the stairs is locked. I put my shoulder to the door. The living room's empty.

'Damnation?'

She appears from the direction of my bedroom. 'Where have you been?' she asks. 'I was looking for you.'

'You had any visitors?'

'Not that I know of.'

I glance at her hands. No cuts, bruising, blood or splinters. 'Hear anything?'

'Not apart from the traffic. But where have you been?'

'It's not where I've been, it's where you were.'

'I wasn't anywhere. What happened?'

I've got to believe her. Correction: I've got to *pretend* I believe her. I tell her what she needs to know, watching her face closely while I say it. But there's no expression on her face, apart from what you'd expect.

'So what do we do now?'

'We sleep – you in your bedroom and me in mine. And after we sleep, we leave the premises and breakfast somewhere on croissants and coffee. Then I do a bit of research while you do some more shopping. After that we meet up again and get out of Paris.'

'I have to sleep in my own room?'

'Yeah, in your own room.'

'But how can I possibly sleep?'

'Just lie down, close your eyes and count corpses. It always works for me.'

As we leave, from behind the closed door of the landlady's room I hear the snuffling of the goat. We find somewhere for breakfast, after which I check out train timetables then look for a gun. But while there are plenty of gunshops in Paris, they all want ID. Showing ID puts Halliwell on a computer, telling the world he's someone with a gun. I don't want to end up on a computer, even as Halliwell. I trawl the dives and speakeasies at the sleazy end of Paris with no result until I bump into a Rasta outside a gunshop.

'What about good manners?' he demands.

This guy's as sensitive as a rat-trap.

'Go entertain the troops in Afghanistan,' I tell him.

'Hey, man, I'm talking about this.' He produces a little black gizmo about the size of a matchbox. 'It opens doors – hence the name: *Good Manners*. See? You place it against a lock, like this.' He places it against the gunshop's lock. 'Then you pull the trigger, like this.' He pulls the trigger. 'And – open Sesame!'

There's no explosion – just a nice, neat hole where the lock used to be. I buy the gizmo, plus the six-pack of charges that comes with it. After which I find myself a hole-in-the-wall internet joint and, using a dead man's email, check all the angles – slave trade, child porn, drugs and prostitution. But none of them fit. By the time I've finished, it's late afternoon. Damnation's waiting at l'Opera where I told her to wait, in the company of our cases and more shopping. I tell her to stuff the shopping in the cases, then I get us to the above-ground railway, via the apartment on the Rue de Rivoli. Where a policewoman's trying to entice the goat with the bloodstained beard into a paddy wagon, only it doesn't want to leave what's left of its mistress …

In Paris there are small stations and there are big ones and Agincourt's one of the big ones. Named after a battle, it looks like the war's still in progress as we drag our bags along the concourse towards the shops.

'Jesus, Rain – or Arthur or Neville or Bruce, or whatever you call yourself,' the dame says, 'I'm not a bloody – dromedary!'

She's dressed in what she must have decided is domestic travel gear – sharp-toed red shoes, a T-shirt so tight you can see her goosebumps, and jeans that look like they've been spray-painted on. She's right, she's not a dromedary. I shake my head.

'What have dromedaries got to do with the price of mangoes?'

'I mean I haven't eaten since – oh, I don't know when – and I'm ravishing.'

Her English could be better but the sentiment works for me. I make way for the marauders milling around us – a yelling, screaming mob all dressed up as rats: preening false whiskers, whisking fake tails, banging drums and waving helium-filled balloons in our faces.

'Who are these idiots?' I shout.

'It's the usual thing,' she shouts back. 'We French are children of the Revolution and if we're not protesting, we're parading. These ones belong to a rugby club called the Rats of Agincourt. But rats to them – I haven't eaten since breakfast and, as I said, I'm ravishing. I'm getting some food.'

I grab a part of her I'm allowed to grab without getting jailed for it.

'Sorry, Damnation. First we got to get tickets.'

I've checked and rechecked the destination on the beggar's ticket and I've also checked the departures board. The dame stops struggling so I let her go.

'Our train leaves at seven,' I say.

I get Damnation into the bureau and tell her to buy two tickets.

'Where to?'

I tell her the wrong place.

'Why me?'

'Look, we're up against professionals. Two of our followers have ended up dead and the concierge just joined them. On my calculation there'll be more and I don't want us to be among them.' I move her towards the counter. 'I didn't talk French before and I still don't talk it now. So you're getting us two one-way tickets to Perpignan.'

After Damnation's bought our tickets, I lead her

back outside. After which we re-enter the office and line up again – only this time separately and apart. And separately and apart we buy two singles to Beguine.

Beguine was the destination written on the ticket in the beggar's wallet, the ticket the man in the Burberry dropped in the cap before slipping through the dog-door and killing the concierge.

And because I figure Beguine's where we'll find Imogene, that's where we're going.

Chapter 27

ESCAPE FROM AGINCOURT

There are half-a-dozen patisseries in the Gare d'Agincourt, but there are still too many rats. When Damnation sees there's a chance she won't be getting any food, she stamps a little foot with an expensive little shoe on it, like she's sick of Paris in general and me in particular.

'How long before our *real* train leaves?'

'Ten minutes.'

She gets her food.

I take the dame and our bags to the wrong platform and together we board the train to Perpignan. After which, using the door-forcer I bought from the Rasta, I force open the door opposite to the one we came in by, the one without a platform, drop the bags on the rails, get down after them, and get the dame down after me.

'What are we doing?'

'We boarded the wrong train and now we're boarding the right one. That means we got to cross the tracks and get ourselves onto the next platform and after that we get down on the rails again then up again and then we board the right train.'

The back door of the right train's locked, but the gizmo does its work again, after which I hoist Damnation up, followed by the bags. I do what I can with the door but it won't lock and the slightest of nudges is going to bust it open. When I straighten, I find Damnation watching me.

'This isn't what I signed up for.'

'You didn't sign up for anything, remember? You wanted to come to France and you wouldn't take no for an answer.'

'That was before and this is now and now I –'

That's as far as she gets before I realise we're being followed by a man in a coat who looks like a ferret, and he's making his way along the platform beside the train, sniffing because he's lost our scent. He could be dismissed as irrelevant. Except for the bulge under the coat, and the sniff.

The starter's whistle sounds. There's the sound of running feet as the train begins to move, the couplings taking up the slack. I get us into the next carriage as behind us I hear the rear door open and half-close. 'Go to the front carriage before the train picks up too much speed.'

After she's gone, I wait for the Ferret. But there's no sign of him – nothing but the hum of wheels gathering speed under us and the rocking of the carriage. He's staying in the back carriage so after ten minutes, I head off after the dame. I don't want a confrontation unless he forces one on me. As I make my way forward, I pass a boy with a balloon he must have nicked from the footy fans, and later on I see the old couple from the Louvre. *They're just on the same journey* … I find Damnation occupying a window seat in the car behind the engine and there's nothing else besides her in the compartment apart from the view, the patisserie and the luggage. I lift the bags onto the luggage rack.

'What was that all about?' Damnation says.

I've seated myself opposite her – I'm facing the way we're going – but only after removing my coat and parking it on the seat. It's smart to have everything secure. These trains go fast. This one starts going fast.

'Someone's out to get me, Damnation, and you invited yourself along for the ride. I don't care how beautiful you are or how upset you get or even how hungry you might become in the process, we're going to find my kid and I'll take care of any problems along the way.' I flick finger against thumb on the hand that's still got the thumb. 'Give me your phone.'

'Why?'

'Because I don't know you from a baguette. We're in the same boat and you could prove to be a leak.' I re-click finger and thumb. 'So – the phone.'

When she shakes her beautiful face, the expression on it is as inscrutable as the Mona Lisa's.

'I'm sorry,' she says, 'but I went to the toilet and the phone fell down the loo.'

Chapter 28

FOR EVERY ACTION ...

I asked for her phone because I want another look at the call log. She might still have the phone, then again she mightn't. Either way, nothing's to be gained from making a song and dance about it, so I keep my trap shut and resist the toe-tap. Instead I stare out the window at scenery that's rapidly changing from the concrete to the ephemeral – from city to towns to villages, from tall buildings to farms – at the same time as I'm keeping an eye on the dame.

I study the timetable they provided with the ticket. It gives the times between stations as well as a handy little diagram showing where the line swerves. *Make sure you're seated on the bends,* the timetable warns, *as well as when the train accelerates immediately afterwards.* I help myself to a crust. When Damnation finishes eating, she wipes her lips with a tissue from her reticule, brushes the crumbs from her lap, and her violet eyes make contact with my ordinary ones.

'I'm sorry about the phone,' she says. 'Losing it might seem an act of sabotage but I assure you it was an accident.' She takes a deep breath. 'Also I don't know if I ever said, but I'm sorry about your daughter.'

After she's got that off her chest, she leans forward and her hands alight on my knees. I don't move. The dame doesn't move her hands, either.

'And now you've got me where you want me,' she says, 'why don't you put me to use?'

'How do you know you're where I want you?'

'Two heads are better than one,' she says.

She takes another deep breath as her body sways with the train.

'I know I'm only here as a profile-changer and perhaps also because I speak French.' Her beautiful eyes fix on mine. 'But I could do a lot better than that.'

She takes her hands off my knees.

'I know you haven't said as much but I think that you *like* me, at least a little bit. You're awkward because I'm a woman. You're afraid of involvements. And maybe you're simply keeping me where you can see me. Yet when you searched my house you came up with zilch and ditto when you went through my bags. You're conflicted. You like me but you also suspect me. You want me to be trustworthy but you think I'm not.' She calms down as fast as she fired up. 'Please believe me, Rainbow, when I say it was a coincidence your Mr Green employed me as a tutor. It was also an accident my phone fell down the toilet. But it's no accident I'm here. You *wanted* me here, remember? But you won't tell me what's going on. For instance, what happened to the man on the plane who later turned up on the Rue de Rivoli? Where did you go while I was taking a shower?

Why did we suddenly leave the flat? And what are we doing on this train? Whatever you believe to the contrary, I *know* I can help you find your daughter.'

It's a long speech and I can't handle long speeches, they've got too many words in them. When she raises her head, her eyes are brimming. Which means the speech didn't only contain a lot of words, there was also emotion. Even more than words, I can't handle emotion.

'What harm can it do?' she says.

I can fight the logic but I'm no match for the eyes. So I tell her about the death of the man in black and also about the gendarmes handing out the cards. I fill her in on the less gory details concerning the concierge, the beggar and the ticket in the wallet. What I don't tell her about is the paper that the rats chewed. Nor that I still don't trust her.

'So that's why we're going to Beguine,' she says. 'But what do you expect to find there?'

According to the guidebook, Beguine's an ancient town on the River Lot, four hours south of Paris. There are a lot of hospitals, a trick clock in the main square and, on a hill overlooking the town, a grand *château* – a big castle – whose owners don't like to be bothered by tourists. I take the question as rhetorical and don't answer it, so Damnation answers it for me.

'You're in two minds about your daughter's disappearance. Is your ex-wife just getting back at you or is this Mr Green up to something? They're not the same thing or even two sides of the same coin. But you know women.'

I don't know women but I nod anyway.

'You'd know, then, that if your ex-wife's intention was to take the child, she'd never signal she was going to do it. Warnings are a male failing, women just do things. So – thinking as a woman – you're right in believing your daughter's removal wasn't an act of revenge.' She pauses. 'Of course, there's always the romance aspect of it. But if it's romance, why take the child? That leaves a third possibility.'

'What possibility's that?'

Damnation shakes her head or maybe the train shakes it for her.

'You know the answer because it's *your* answer – that Mr Green took them for his own nefarious purposes.'

She looks uncertain – or maybe it's troubled – as if she's had second or even third thoughts about the wisdom of saying too much. There's something going on and I don't know what it is. It's always like that where dames are concerned but this is even more so. 'Your ex-wife – what's her name? Praline.' She says it *pray lean*; I correct her: *Salina*. 'All right, Salina. Well, she's a mother, not a monster. Which leaves a fourth possibility: that Mr Green's escaping something – maybe an ex-wife – and, like you, he simply needs a profile-changer.'

'I'm sorry, Damnation. Green cleaned both the house in Sydney and the flat in Paris too well to be anything but a pro. Also we've been followed too well for this to be anything other than a pro operation. My aunt was mugged, a dancer was killed and three more corpses have followed hard on the heels of the first.'

'It still could be just a coincidence ...' she murmurs.

I trot out my hard line. 'I don't believe in coincidences.'

You rely a lot on reflection in this game, which is why I'm facing the way the train's going. Everything in the corridor is reflected in the wall behind the dame. That's how I see the figure and that's why I hurl myself into the corridor. Only to find – nothing. Nothing apart from the lurching corridor of a high-speed train plus the certain knowledge that a moment ago someone was standing there. I wasn't going after him unless he came after me. But now …

'What is it?' the dame asks.

It's an eight-car train and it's no more than five minutes to the next station so I don't reply. Instead I head back through the train. By the time I reach the second car, there's only three minutes, thirty-seven seconds left to check the final six carriages. Some cars are compartmentalised. The others are in a two-by-two seat-conformation on either side of a narrow aisle. It's not easy staying balanced. An unexpected corner could land me flat on my face. Ditto unexpected braking and acceleration. In the second car a student's reading about the 1986 destruction of the nuclear reactor at Chernobyl while a nerd's peering through thick-lensed glasses at the kid with the balloon.

The train accelerates suddenly. I've anticipated it and brace. Predictably the kid topples onto his mother while the balloon escapes from his grasp. But unpredictably the balloon doesn't float to the ceiling. Instead it slams against the back of the carriage.

'Incredible!' the nerd says. 'A perfect example of Roemer's Law of Relativity. When the train accelerates, the balloon doesn't hit the train. Instead the train speeds forward and hits the balloon!'

But the mother's got her own law.

She whacks the kid.

Chapter 29

... THERE'S AN EQUAL AND OPPOSITE REACTION

The third and fourth cars are full of innocence. Passengers sleeping, passengers talking, passengers reading. There could be nothing or there could be anything. And I'm prepared for anything as I work my way through the carriages, carding my way into locked toilets when I have to and remembering to grab the overhead rail well before the train takes a turn for the worse at 200 miles an hour.

The old folks from the Louvre are asleep in the fifth car. The dining car's closed. In the sixth is a man in a wheelchair. One carriage and one minute, fifty-three seconds to go.

I enter the last car.

Gripping the overhead rack I glance around. Three passengers occupy the carriage.

First passenger: seated halfway along the carriage to my left, empty bottle between legs. Correction: not sitting – sprawling. Red-faced, faded-pink scarf around neck, no marked characteristics and seemingly dead to all around him. Not the Ferret.

Second passenger: further along the carriage, occupying a seat on the opposite side to the red-faced man. Younger, paler, sneering. Smaller than the first man and therefore in the ballpark. I consider taking him but before I do that, I check the last passenger. Always check the last passenger.

He's the last man standing, a small, thin figure in a gabardine overcoat at the other end of the aisle, his back to the door that we all entered the train by – the one that won't lock properly because I blew a hole in the lock. As the train slows for a corner, he grabs the back of a seat with one hand, while the other hand reaches for the bulge in the Burberry. My man.

Ninety seconds before the train docks. One and a half minutes before the Ferret can discreetly slip off the train after murdering me and just as discreetly slip back on again. One minute, twenty seconds.

The aisle restricts movement. There's no room for fancy footwork. And I'm not armed while the Ferret is. I couldn't carry a gun on the plane because it's not allowed and I couldn't buy one in Paris because it would put me on a computer. And being on a computer is like being at one end of a carriage on a high-speed train with a killer at the other end going for his gun. There's not much future in it.

In this game you expect the unexpected. And the unexpected is the young man with the sneer leaping to his feet as the train emerges from the corner. I mistook the look. It wasn't a sneer but a look of apprehension. He's holding one hand to his mouth while the other hand's scrabbling for a hold. Only there isn't one. He's on the loose, the thrust of the train's post-corner acceleration sending him skidding down the aisle towards the Ferret, and for a nanosecond the Ferret's distracted. The aisle skims under the sick man. I do a demi-plie and take to the air. The acceleration does the rest. It's the law of relativity in motion. For once, I go with the law.

The revolver the Ferret's gripping is a Manurhin MR73 – a French-made .357 Magnum – short and sweet and much favoured by the gendarmerie as well as by marksmen the world over. But the best's not good enough in a high-speed train bearing you swiftly towards an airborne attacker. The Ferret's slugs go wide, ricocheting off the chromework and into seats. I count three. That leaves three, four if there was already one in the chamber. The Ferret doesn't get a chance to unleash the rest. He utters a sound like a knifed tyre as the train thrusts his face into my fist and his back against the door that we came in by, the one that no longer locks ...

I grip the toilet handle as the back door flies open on a vista of high-speed train line fringed by hay bales. The rails reach up as hungry as Death. With my free hand, I make a grab for the Ferret as he scrabbles to stay alive. The gun clatters to the floor and the Ferret's mouth is a gaping hole. But like the man in the painting in the Louvre, no sound emerges as the Ferret flies out and bounces once, twice, three times, and the hay bales around him scatter like straws in the wind.

I turn to find the young man being sick and the red-faced man waking, his empty bottle rolling forward as the train slows for the next-to-last station. The toilet door opens and a surprised face peers out. I nod, retrieve the gat and pocket it, then make my way back through the train. The old couple in the fifth car are still asleep. And in the third, the kid's contemplating a scrap of blue plastic, all that's left of his balloon.

Chapter 30

BEGIN THE BEGUINE

When I get back to Damnation she still looks beautiful. She also looks guilty. I shift my coat off the seat, at the same time as I reach for the guide to Beguine.

'I don't suppose you're going to tell me where you were,' she says.

She's too calm, an expletive in the making. Never excite the expletives.

'Just seeing a man about a dog.'

Guilt and calmness are dangerous bedfellows.

'I've always thought that to be such a stupid expression,' she mutters, pulling her legs up on the seat under her. 'It's so illogically English – or in your case, Australian. Oh, I know it means you've been to the lavatory. But why a dog, for heaven's sake? Why not a horse or a cow or a – a ferret?'

The violet eyes are guileless. Gripping onto the book, I look out the window as the crops, cows and pasture grass hurtle back in the direction of Paris.

'Anyhow,' she goes on, 'you were gone too long for a toilet run, and one of your hands is swollen. So you didn't go to the loo. You wanted to escape. You find me an encumbrance and a nag.' She glances at the suitcases then back again. 'I'm just another piece of baggage and you wish I weren't here.'

'If wishes were dishes I'd be working in a scullery.'

The nonsense gets Damnation smiling but she refuses to go along with the smile.

'Another one of your stupidities.' She leans forward. 'But tell me – before you went off to do whatever you did, you were saying that you believed your daughter was abducted ...'

Some questions aren't what they seem and this is one of them. The conversation isn't about the kid, it's about me. 'I'm playing it by ear.'

'Another one of your stupid expressions.'

Daylight's fading. So, too, is hope. *Why was Imogene taken?* I could be on a wild-goose chase. The kid mightn't be in France at all. And even if she is, we're headed south when she could be east, north, west, or north-by-northwest. But – the man in black was after me when he got hit by the bus, the dead beggar had a ticket to Beguine, the Ferret killed the concierge after she blabbed, and I know –

But what do I know? Little more than the fact I've got to park the paranoia. They were only cops handing out tickets. And the Ferret mightn't have been tailing me – just another tourist on the same journey. *No, no and no again.* I'm headed for the right place all right. It's just a matter of what I'll find when I get there. I tear my attention away from the castle, the one whose owners don't care to be bothered by tourists, and open the guidebook.

When they begin the Beguine
It brings back the sound of music so tender,
It brings back a night of tropical splendour

It brings back a memory ever green …
It's not what's written in the guidebook.
But it's what I read.

When we arrive at Beguine the rain's set in with a vengeance and I can see a troop of what look like soldiers working its way through a vineyard towards the château. They must be hunters because this is France and people hunt here. I drag my eyes away, shove the guidebook back in my pocket, retrieve the cases and climb onto the platform after the dame. She's nervous and the nervousness features in her word placement.

'Do you get the follow we're being feelinged?'

'You mean the *feeling* we're being *followed*.'

She glances behind, shivering.

'So you're experiencing it, too – that *follow*?'

Among our fellow passengers, the two old folks are struggling with their bags while further off a figure darts behind a bus with *TOULOUSE* written in its destination window. He could be anyone or nobody. I've turned one shadow into a corpse. All that's left now is a bunch of tourists, among them the old couple, Harold and Maud. A helicopter swings across the evening sky, heading north. The rain's hammering down and as we head uphill towards town, Damnation's dainty new parasol affords as much protection as a periwinkle in a deluge.

'Where are we staying?' she asks.

'Not at a hotel for a start.'

'Why not at a hotel for a start?'

'Because hotels put your passport details into a computer. And when they do that, people know where we are – that is, if they don't know already.'

Damnation tries to avoid a rush of water from a drainpipe but isn't quick enough. 'So-where-are-we-staying-if-not-in-a-hotel?'

The guidebook says Beguine's on a pilgrim track and that there's plenty of suitable accommodation. Tell that to the cherries. Because apart from the hotels there seems to be nothing. Until a voice behind us says, 'We know somewhere.'

I push Damnation out of the way, drop the cases, go down on one knee and go for the gat. But it's only the old couple – Maud clutching a big red, white and blue umbrella, while Harold's in charge of the bags. I leave the gun in its garage and help Damnation to her feet.

'Where?'

'Jaqui's place.'

It looks like the journey we're on is about to get even more similar.

Chapter 31

LETTERS ON A TABLECLOTH

The bike's an old Birmingham Small Arms Sloper – commonly known as a BSA – the kind that despatch riders rode between trenches when wars were wars, with the familiar girder fork straddling the front wheel, a wide saddle seat, arm-stretch handlebars and a sidecar. It's standing outside a tall, skinny joint that, if it were any taller and skinnier, would qualify as a chimney.

A sign says *BUTTERFLIES ARE BEAUTIFUL* and a ring on the bell brings us Jaqui, a dame with a voice that's swing-song. And while Damnation brushes herself down and the codgers stand around looking gormless, I check out our surroundings. The ground floor's one room. It contains a table, the beginnings of a narrow staircase, and too many walking shoes smelling of gruyere. Apart from the dame and the shoes, there's a gnome on the grave-side of ninety wearing a forage suit and a limp. For some reason he zeroes in as soon as he sees me, rapping my chest like he's tapping ashes.

'Listen up stranger and listen up good. Jaqui's my granddaughter and anyone wanting to mess with her climbs over my dead body to do it. Plus the bodies of my friends and the bodies of *their* friends. Read me, stranger?'

He smells of past apprehensions and incipient madness. I tell him I read him like a *Tin Tin* comic.

Jaqui interposes. 'Why don't I show you to your rooms? Don't mind Grandpa,' she adds as she precedes us up the stairs. 'He's got certain – passions. He hates aristocrats, for instance – or anyone who thinks they *own* people. In the Second World War he was in charge of the local Resistance. His wife – my grandmother – was killed by the Germans in retaliation for his activities, leaving a tiny baby – our mother. My sister and I are rather precious to him – hence his behaviour.'

She changes the subject abruptly.

'As to the accommodation,' she lowers her swing-song voice, 'we normally only put up people like the old couple, so there are no double beds.'

I tell her that suits me fine. Jaqui leaves the codgers on the third floor and takes us past a share bathroom to the fifth. Our room's the size of a dishrag and Jaqui knocks against me during a tight manoeuvre. I wince and she looks down, her eyes widening.

'Oh dear, look at your poor hand. How did that happen?'

I tell her I cut myself shaving.

'But it should be seen to. My sister's a nurse ...' Her eyes turn shifty and she stares at me confused while her hands flutter to her face like a pair of waterlogged butterflies.

'I'm sorry, sometimes I get nervous and talk too much. Here I am blabbing all the town's secrets when you could be anybody.'

She's scared of something. It might be the old man. Then again, it mightn't be. I treat her apology like the soup the town's famous for and park it on the backburner.

After the dame leaves, Damnation gets a look on her face that says the room's small. 'The room's small,' she says, as if the look mightn't be enough; she makes one of those gestures people make when a room's small. 'For instance, where am I supposed to change?'

'Try the share bathroom. From what I saw, right now it's not being shared.'

She opens her case, grabs some clothes and flounces out the door, and when she gets back we go out for something to eat.

Anywhere else but in France, the eatery the swing-song dame directs us to would qualify as a hole in the wall. It contains a small table, a red gingham cloth on the table, and a candle on the cloth. I decide on the wine and the dame opts for a confession.

'While you were seeing a – man about a dog, or whatever it was – I happened to look in the lining of your hat. Where I discovered – this.'

She's changed into a little blue number with a neckline so low it stretches the definition, not to mention the neckline. She produces from the neckline the rat-chewed scraps of glossy paper bearing the letters that might spell *G-R-E-E-N*.

'Why were you looking in my hat?'

'What's sauce for the gander –' She pauses midstream and decides to paddle back. 'Please don't be angry. After all, you did search my house in Sydney and after that, my case. And when I went shopping in Paris, you followed me.' As if to distract attention from what she just said, she leans forwards and taps the paper. 'I saw you examining this on the plane. What's so important about it?'

The wine comes and we order our meal – oysters in the natural for Damnation and leek soup for me. She forks up an oyster. There were local numbers on her call log when I checked it in Paris. But she's French so it could be family. Apart from which she's beautiful. So over the soup I tell her about the rat paper and when I finish she's nodding over her wine.

'When I found the paper I knew it was significant or you wouldn't have hidden it. So I spread it out and thought I – saw something.'

'What was that something?'

The restaurant's dark but I can still see her expression and it's troubled. She shuffles the pieces of paper around before glancing at me out of her beautiful eyes. 'What's the difference between boys and girls?'

I know what it is but figure Damnation might have her own angle. I'm right. She does.

'The difference is that, while boys are outside smacking the heads off daisies, girls are inside playing with bits of paper.' When she sits back the candlelight resumes its dance on the parts of her that aren't in the dress. 'When I was a little girl I used to do origami. I know my way around paper.'

She's ordered frogs' legs and paté – the mashed-up liver of force-fattened geese – while I've got the salad. She deals herself a forkful of paté. I pour her more wine.

'So what does the paper tell you?'

'It doesn't tell me anything – yet. I'm simply saying that it might. For instance, I know where the letters were and how many spaces there were between them. And knowing that gives me a clue to the words.' She absorbs more wine and her violet eyes become even more violet as she shuffles the paper.

'Even with the pieces separated,' she continues, 'I can see that three of the letters were consecutive ones in the same word. Which gives us *G-R-E*.'

I munch on a lettuce leaf.

'That leaves two letters unaccounted for.'

'Yes, the *E* and the *N*.' Damnation sits back. She's finished her oysters, frogs' legs and paté and demolished a fair swag of the wine, and now she's going to tell me about the *E* and the *N*. 'On my estimate there were six – perhaps seven – letters between the *G-R-E* and the last *E*.'

'Are you sure?'

She nods.

'Pretty sure.'

'What else are you pretty sure of?'

'That there wasn't much space between the last *E* and the *N* – if there was any at all.'

'So in the words of a crossword enthusiast, we got *G*, *R*, *E*, something, something, something, something,

something, something, followed by something else. Then there's an *E*, maybe something, and finally an *N*.' I look up. 'Anything else?'

'I'm sorry but if there is something, I can't see it.'

I rake up the scraps and put them back in the hat before Damnation can swipe them again. She's a help but she's also no help at all. I can trust her and I can't trust her in the slightest. Over coffee, I don't know what else to say so I deal her an aphorism.

'In this world, all that people like me have are the scraps left by the rats.'

Chapter 32

WHAT THE NEWSPAPER SAID

The moon cuts a swathe across the room and the gap between our beds is an unbridgeable chasm. I've never slept with this dame before and I'm not sleeping with her now. Sleep's out of the question. She's muttering too much, her voice competing with the moon and the moon coming light years second.

It's like she's doing battle with the Devil and the Devil's got all the ammunition. I feel sorry for her but pity's not going to rescue Imogene. Then I get a brainwave, courtesy of what she's muttering: What if the words aren't English – but Latin, Double Dutch or Swahili? I try half-a-dozen languages and I'm still trying when the village bells toll the *angelus* and the dame stretches, revealing the fact that she sleeps in much the same state as her oysters.

'I had such a wonderful rest,' she says, smiling across the chasm separating our beds.

I'm pleased that somebody did.

A brace of triple-smack coffees puts me right, or as right as I'm ever going to be after a night like that. I've reshaved my head and I'm wearing what an accountant might wear, while Damnation's got on a Galeries Lafayette T-shirt with the words *Le Sacre du Printemps* – Rite of Spring – scrawled on the front and jeans that are even tighter than the T-shirt. We're seated in the usual cane chairs at the usual cane table on the usual potholed French footpath when she squeals, causing me to look at her even more closely than I was already.

She's clutching a copy of the local rag – *Lot-Matin* – and from where I'm sitting there's a photo of someone presenting the local Mayor with a cheque. Next to it is another story entitled: *WHERE ARE THEY NOW?* And that's the story I study while Damnation holds up the paper. 'A man fell off a train yesterday,' she reads. 'A farmer fossicking on the tracks found him. If he hadn't stumbled across him, the man would still be lying there, unattended.'

I shake off a bad feeling. What do they mean – *unattended?*

'Where's the body now?'

The dame rustles the paper for a better look. The story's just letters but they're letters that are joined together. 'What body? There *is* no body – at least not in the sense *you*'d use the word. The man's still alive.'

'How can a man survive a fall out of the back of a high-speed train?'

When Damnation looks up from the newspaper, she's frowning. Maybe it's the sun.

'It says he owes his life to the presence of some hay bales beside the track …'

I remember the hay bales.

'Where is he now?'

'In hospital, why?' The dame takes a beautiful hand away from the blatt and brings it up to her mouth. 'Oh, my God! He fell off *our* train, didn't he?' She stares at me. 'And *you* did it! *You* pushed him!'

She drags her eyes away from mine and back to the blatt.

'They even say as much: *Police are looking for a man who eyewitnesses say was on the train at the time.* There's even a description of the gun – a Manchurian something-or-other. *If seen do not approach. Instead contact the following number.*'

'What's the following number?'

Damnation tells me but I already know what it is. It's the one on the cards the cop was handing out in the Rue de Rivoli. The section that handles business that's too hot for the rest of the gendarmerie to handle. Like armed assassins getting chucked out of high-speed trains.

'There's even an e-fit or com-fit or something of the suspect. And if it's not you, it's your daily double.'

The sick passenger mustn't have been so sick and/or the red-faced man so wasted that they … Then there was the face coming out of the toilet. Together they must have come up with a description.

'Do they mention you?' I ask.

'What do you mean?'

I take it slower.

'Do they say this suspect of theirs might have been in the company of a woman?'

Damnation shakes her head like she can't shake anything else, so I shake it for her.

'That means we're stuck with each other, Damnation.' I don't wait for her to object. 'They're looking for a big, bald joker and you're a profile-changer. Of course, you could get away from me and blab but then they'd just make you an accessory before, after or during the fact. So sticking with me is your only option.' I leave the words hanging. 'Where did they take him?'

'To the hospital.'

'Do they say *which* hospital?'

Damnation shakes her head.

I settle my hat on my bald pate, climb to my feet, drop a handful of euros on the table and, just as I turn to leave, glimpse a shadow near the monkeys in the joke clock in the square.

'Where are we going?' the dame asks.

'To see a woman about a hospital.'

Jaqui knows enough and she's prepared to share it. She's naturally chatty. It's like it's only the presence of the old man that turns her into a clam.

'There are a number of hospitals in the area, all catering for different needs. Patients come here from all over. You might have noticed the helicopters – they fly patients to and from Paris. Among the facilities are the Beguine General, the Silicone Private and the Mon Dieu Hospice for the Dying. Not to mention the Infirmarie Speciale.' She pauses

as if considering what she's saying before rushing on.
'There's even a suggestion that the château ...'
'What château?'
The swing-song voice turns cautious.
'The – château that you – might have seen from
the train. Grandpa says ...'
'What does Grandpa say?'
Like a small yacht in an unpredictable wind she
changes tack again.
'He says that – loose lips lose wars ...'
'What wars would they be?'
'Grandpa's own personal war, I suppose.'
She's trying to tell me something other than what
it looks like she's saying.
'Where do they take people who fall out of trains?'
'My guess would be the General.'

Me and Damnation take a lunch of baguette, cheese
and the local black wine high into the limestone
hills by the river. Across the river, past the town,
the château stands proud upon its hill. The General
Hospital's in the valley, a road leading down to it
from the château. I examine the road and the castle,
followed by the hospital. The spring sunshine's
warm. The dame takes a nap and after I finish my
examination of the landscape I join her in La-La
Land. It's late afternoon before we get going again.
We take a circuitous route, one that takes us past
the castle, and when we finally reach the hospital,
Damnation's carrying her new shoes and there's

only an hour to nightfall. I nod towards a bunch of rosebushes.

'If we get separated, we meet back here.'

There's three ways of playing this. I could send the dame on a reconnaissance, we could make like we're part of the scenery, or I could take my chances. I still don't trust her and I'm too big to merge, so I chance it, nodding to doctors, patients and nurses as I push open the doors, motioning Damnation to follow.

'If anyone asks, we're just visiting,' I say as we enter.

'Why? What are you going to do?'

I don't tell her what I'm going to do because I still don't trust her. Part of me says I'm going to find out what the Ferret knows, while the other part – the part with brains in it – tells me there'll be too many police around to get the chance.

It doesn't mean I'm not going to try.

Chapter 33

RUNNING INTERFERENCE

Hospitals are hospitals and the General's no exception. We pass a lot of doctors, a couple of guards and too many signs. There's something wrong.

'Where's the Emergency department, Damnation?'

'Along there somewhere – I think …'

She's both right and wrong at the same time. 'You might *think* you're right,' I tell her. 'But my feeling is it's not that way at all, it's along here.'

We go through a doorway and are immediately accosted by a guard.

'What do you think you're doing?'

I'm pressing a nerve at the side of his neck, that's what I'm doing. And after I've done that I pull one of his eyelids back to check how long he'll be asleep and calculate we've got ten minutes, give or take an eyelid flutter. I shove him in a laundry cupboard.

'Merde!' the dame says.

It comes out sounding like 'murder'.

We're in a corridor that's wide enough to drive a bed through, with too many doors leading off it and too many cops at the other end. I pull Damnation into a room containing fresh linen and bedpans, to the accompaniment of a sound like thunder. 'What's that?' Damnation asks.

'A helicopter. We're in a hospital where they bring patients from Paris, and after they've fixed them fly them back again.' I grab her arm. 'Now listen, you're going to run interference.'

'Murder,' she says again.

I grab her arm. 'Know what that is?'

'Yes, it's when people interfere with other people, the way you're interfering with me now.'

I let her go.

'It's an American football term referring to a ploy whereby a player distracts another player or players, enabling a fellow team member to score. *Interference* is when you get in people's way.' I indicate the cops at the other end of the hallway.

'You're going to get in their way; you're going to faint in front of the fuzz.'

'I could faint right now.'

'Hold onto that thought.'

I grab a handful of pamphlets out of a dispenser on the wall for cover, and step out of the room as Damnation heads down the hall. I watch her crumple.

The cops yell simultaneously and simultaneously they go to her rescue. But there's too much French gallantry and they fumble the catch and the dame goes down, creating enough confusion for me to get along the corridor, cramming the pamphlets into the pocket with the gun in it as I go, following the signs to Casualty. In the first room I draw a blank. The second contains a kid. Room number three produces a dame that looks like she's got the plague. Four's empty. Five's my man.

There are two beds. I get myself to the one containing the Ferret. He's got cuts and contusions from head to toe, his head's bandaged, and he's got as many tubes coming out of him as Aunt Rube. His eyes stare from gaps in the bandages. Killers don't like being on the receiving end. He knows who I am and the fear in his eyes is palpable. I lean over him to maintain the fear.

'Can you talk?'

'No,' he says.

'Then you're going to die.' The tubes wriggle as he shakes his head, while from outside comes the sound of the gendarmes trying to breathe life back into the dame. I grab one of the tubes.

'No!' the Ferret says again, only this time with more feeling.

'Then tell me where I'll find my daughter.'

Confusion replaces the fear.

'What daughter? What the hell are you on about? I don't know any daughters!'

His voice possesses a nasal quality, partly on account of the tubes, but mostly because of the fear.

'Why did you kill the *concierge*?' I demand. 'And why were you following me, armed with a gun?'

He ignores the first question – which means he's not denying it – but answers the second.

'Because they paid me to follow you.'

'That's not good enough.'

The bruise over his eye has turned a nice shade of yellow and someone's daubed the wound down his cheek with gerundial violet. I rip out a tube.

'But that's all they told me!'

I reach for another tube.

'Who's *they*?'

What I can see of his forehead creases until it looks like a condensed version of the tracks he landed on and his carved-up mouth trembles.

'I don't know, honest I don't! The organisation's big and they keep us in what they call information cells. I know only what they think I need to know.'

I'm having trouble making sense of what he's telling me past his fear, the noise of the machine and the efforts of the gendarmes in the hallway.

'And what did you *need* to know?'

'I was to report on your movements. After you left Paris but before you got to Beguine.'

'Why did you do it?'

'For very big dough.'

Hoofs hammer our way. The cops can smell a rat. I lean over the Ferret.

'Sorry I nearly killed you.'

He looks relieved.

'That's all right.'

'You misunderstand me. What I'm saying is I'm sorry I didn't succeed.' The lines on the screen on the machine beside him say I came close. 'My being sorry can be taken two ways.'

He nods but it's the end of the interview. I dive into the other bed and I've just pulled up the covers as the gendarmes enter.

'He's still here,' one says, looking at the Ferret.

'And still alive.'

'We'd better get back to madame.'

They get back to madame. Only she's not there when they get back to her. Instead, she's where I told her to be, huddled among the rosebushes.

'Nice faint,' I tell her.

She manages a ragged smile.

'That's because it was real. What have you got in your pocket?'

I pull out the pamphlets.

'I picked them up as cover while you were fainting.' She takes the pamphlets while I squint at the building. 'How many floors are there?'

'I don't know. Why?'

'Because something's not right.'

Chapter 34

THE SCARLET LETTER

We're in a ditch beside the vineyard on the same hill as the château. There's just enough light to see by. In the distance I hear sirens. I consider our position. We can't show our faces in daylight because someone might recognise us. By now, the Ferret will have told the cops I tried to murder him a second time. My description's in the papers and before nightfall will also be on every gendarmerie computer in France – in company with a description of the dame. Headed: *The Bald and the Beautiful.*

'Listen to this!' Damnation's staring at one of the pamphlets. 'Human organ transplant has come a long way since Christiaan Barnard performed the first successful heart transplant in South Africa fifty years ago. Surgeons are now at the cutting edge of achieving it, it's just a matter of ethics and finding suitable donors.'

I've got a stone in my shoe. I bend to get it out.

'Listen!' Damnation's out of the foxhole, thrusting the pamphlet in my face and shouting. 'It says here: *Greffe du rein.* Now tell me the meaning of *greffe du rein.*'

I'm no longer pretending I don't know French. 'It

means *kidney transplant.*' I say it slow. 'That's what my aunt needs. So what? I can't see what that's got to do with –'

But the dame's on a rock 'n' roll. 'Look at the heading again,' she urges. 'The first three letters in particular. Then skip five – no, seven – spaces. Now – ignoring the letter *i* which, typographically, is so narrow that it hardly counts – and what's left?'

The foxhole's suddenly claustrophobic. I'm finding it hard to breathe.

'G-R-E-E-N.' Even then I don't budge – I made much the same out of what the air-waitress said: GREeat trip ENjoy. 'It could be a coincidence ...'

Damnation shakes her head.

'I thought you didn't do coincidences.' She grabs more pamphlets out of my fist. 'Look at this! *Greffe du poumon* – that's lung transplant; *greffe du foie* – that's liver, what I had for dinner last night; *greffe* whatever you want; *greffe du tissu* – that's human tissue; *greffe du coeur* – that's –'

But she doesn't need to say any more. *WHERE ARE THEY?* ran the newspaper heading. And while we sat in the sun and Damnation read about the Ferret falling out of the train I was reading what could be Imogene's last testament and obituary: *To date, 73 residents of Beguine and surrounds are unaccounted for. Too many are missing. It's as if a flying saucer comes out of the sky and carries them off to Mars ...* The sirens grow louder. Soon there'll body-heat detectors, tracker dogs and a bunch of hunters like I the ones I saw from the train. It's only a matter of time. But we haven't got time. I grab the pamphlets, tracking the words in each one to the bitter end. And at the end is the face of an ordinary-looking man whose distinguishing feature is his handsomeness – that plus the hand that's passing a cheque to the mayor like he's never stopped handing out cheques: a strong hand. I drag out the rat scraps and place them over the kidney pamphlet. Even the paper's the same.

I ball up the scraps as a helicopter clatters overhead. There's none so blind as those who can't see what's right in front of their noses. The chopper's lights are on, revealing that it's a stretch job. I haven't come to the wrong place at all. Au contraire, I'm right at the heart of the right place. The question is whether I'm too late to do anything about it.

'I've got to go,' I tell the dame.

'I'm coming with you.'

'I'll be faster without you.'

'It's not just about *fast*. You're a man on the run and I'm a profile-changer. I know now that you know French but I can still help you. And you're going to need all the help you can get. Where are we going?'

'To see a man.'

'About a dog?'

'Not this time, Damnation. This man's got a lot more going for him than just a dog.'

I finally get the stone out of my shoe. But as we get ourselves back to town, I'm thinking I should have left it where it was, and worn it like a hairshirt.

Chapter 35

WHERE LOYALTIES LIE

The motorcycle's still outside the Butterfly House and Le Patron's still old. He's also still angry.

'You – foreigner! Why do you insist on hanging around my girls?'

I hold up my hands, palms outwards to indicate the absence of weapons.

'I'm not here for your family,' I say. 'I'm here for you.'

On the wall behind the old man hangs a sepia photograph of half-a-dozen young men – some in rough uniform, one wearing roll-legged shorts, all grim-faced for the camera, clutching an assortment of weaponry – squatting in front of or leaning against the selfsame bike that's outside the Butterfly House. The old man sees what I'm looking at and laughs.

'Yes, that's me. I'm the young one in the middle wearing the officer's cap and holding the .303. And while my body parts might have been of use to you then, Monsieur, they are no longer. My organs have been well and truly shot to pieces by my very great age and the war.'

I shake my head.

'I'm not after your organs, Patron. I'm after your assistance.'

'Resistance?'

'That, too. Trust me, I'm not *with* them, I'm *against* them. And I believe you can help me.'

I wait while he computes what I just told him. He won't have seen the WANTED poster. When you get to a certain age, news ceases to be of interest. But not everything doesn't interest him and when Damnation smiles her encouragement, the old man finally relents.

'All right, I believe you're not one of them,' he replies. 'But if you're not, who are you, why are you here, and what do you want from me?'

He's asking questions within questions, like he already knows the answers but needs to be sure I know what he wants me to understand. And suddenly I sense something about this old man I haven't realised before. It's not just the quizzical expression on his face. We're talking French but it's not that, either. It's the sense that there's something terribly wrong with him. But it's too late to turn back. So I answer the questions.

'I'm a detective who's also a father looking for his daughter. You said *they*. Well, we both know who *they* are. They're the people who've taken my daughter, threatening to do to her what you've always feared they might do to Jaqui here. I've got to rescue my daughter and I believe you can help me do it.'

'How much do you know?' the old man asks.

He listens intently while I talk and at the end he seems to trust me. A lot more than I trust him.

'All right, I'm satisfied you're not one of them,' he says. 'Now I'll tell you who *they* are because I don't think you fully realise.' He pauses, during which I see him glance at Jaqui. 'They're people who think some lives are worth more than others.' He pauses again, as if there's a complex idea to get across and he wants to ensure he gets it across right. 'It's what we fought against in the Revolution, and it's the same thing we battled in the 1940s. A sense of superiority.' Stray thoughts seem to pass and re-pass through his mind. 'Now we have these people. They call themselves Hearts and Minds, a euphemism for the illegal obtaining and transplantation of body parts. And just like the aristocrats in the Revolution and after that the Germans in the war they'll stop at nothing to attain their ends.'

There are wheels within wheels here – like with the monkey clock in the town square – a merging and coalescing behind the simplicity of the hands telling the time on the face of the clock. It's like a multiplicity of ideas is all mixed up in the old man's head, driving his obsession.

'Our enemy does transplants. In the safety of our homes we laugh and call them The Organ Grinders: those, nice, innocent little musical-perambulator people you see in the street. But *outside* our homes we don't dare to call them anything. We have families, you see. It's just like it was in the war. Our families are under constant threat.'

The old man clasps and unclasps his useless-for-transplant hands while his mind undergoes similar convulsions.

'They get their product – their organs for

transplant – on the black market. People sell themselves or they sell others to put food on the table. Or the Organ Grinders just help themselves …' The old man's mouth twists and lines cross and recross his face like lasers with too many targets. 'Donors are kidnapped in America, Europe, Africa, Asia – yes, even in Australia. A potential donor is identified and, after that, if approved either by the recipient or the recipient's family, their organs are – I believe the word's *harvested*. If the transplant results in the death of the donor, the remains are discreetly disposed of.'

The old soldier's mouth trembles. He's at war again. But it's like he's at war with himself.

'Do you understand me? The closest parallel is when aristocrats exploited the peasants before the French Revolution in 1789.' He seems to be struggling to untangle different thoughts. 'Sometimes the donors are tricked into co-operating. There are so-called "honey traps", in which people are offered sex or free plane tickets to La Belle France. The victims don't realise the tickets are one-way until too late.'

When the old man pours himself another coffee, a lot ends up in his saucer. And when he drinks from the saucer, even more spills on the table.

'Organs can be removed in situ, to be shipped off to their destination in suitable containers. Or bodies are sent complete – that is, drugged, duped or already dead. The business requires the connivance of powerful people, whose loved ones receive free transplants. Or they just get money – there's a lot of bribery and corruption of police and politicians. It's

like it was in the Revolution and again in the war —
we no longer know who our friends are.' He pauses.
'In the end, what we cling onto is what's best for our
families.'

After that there's silence — too much silence.
Which is finally broken by Damnation asking,
shakily, 'But all this buying of organs and bribing
must cost millions. Where does the money come
from?'

'We're talking about a multi-billion-euro-a-year
industry. On the white market in Australia alone
doctors pay $10,000 for an aortic valve. But on
the black market it's far different, because they're
no longer buying generic. Select kidneys sell for
100,000 euros while handpicked hearts go for as
much as a million. You see, people like to keep their
loved ones alive ...'

There's still something horribly wrong about what
the old man's saying and the way he's saying it. Like
there's something he's trying to convince himself of.

'You're a detective, so you'll already know that
many people around here have gone missing. That's
why I keep a close eye on my girls. When you turned
up I thought you were one of them. There was no
trust in the Revolution or again in the war. It's the
same now. In your grey suit, big hat and tie, you
clearly weren't a tourist. So I had you tailed from the
moment you arrived.'

'Was the man on the train one of yours?'

'If you mean by that the one in the hospital, no.
He's one of theirs and he was meant to stop you.'

'How do you know that?'

The old man's eyes waver before hardening.

'I learnt a lot in the war, Monsieur, just as I did from reading about the Revolution. And first and foremost I learnt the importance of survival – of oneself but also the survival of one's family.' He shunts back to the main line. 'Worldwide, traffickers harvest 20,000 kidneys annually. Apart from kidneys, bodies contain lungs, livers, pancreases, bones, tissue and hearts. Transplants occur in the US, Spain, Russia, Serbia, Kosovo – and here.'

'And where are these operations performed, in France?'

The old man glances at Jaqui, who quickly looks away. He turns back to me and, as he does so, he takes a deep, quavering breath. It's like all his past and all his future and all his family's past and future as well as the past and future of the whole of France are in that breath.

'At the château.'

Chapter 36

TONIGHT JOSEPHINE

For a long time after the old man finishes speaking, silence reigns. Clearly distressed, Jaqui excuses herself and goes upstairs, leaving the old man gazing lovingly after her. After which he collects himself. He seems to have come to a decision.

'Very well, Monsieur,' he says. 'We will help you.'

He limps to a cupboard, pulls it open, lifts out an old-fashioned military field telephone, and brings it to the table. He dials a number, someone answers, and he speaks softly into the mouthpiece.

'Hello, darling? It's Grandpa. I need confirmation of what you told me earlier … I thought so. Very well, we must move. The castle … Yes, I said the castle.' I sense resistance at the other end but the old man's adamant. 'He's a detective and we've got no choice … Yes, they've got his daughter … I'm doing what I believe is for the best … You will activate the phone tree and afterwards come here … Yes, all of them … I love you, ma cherie.'

When he's finished, he carefully replaces the handset and resumes our conversation as if the phonecall never happened. 'Because I'm egalitarian – all right, a communist – I hate castles and all they represent. I hate the transplant people for much the same reason. Both these hatreds are now combined in the one target. It's ironic.'

The old fighter might be speaking French, but he's wrong in any language.

'Not *ironic*,' I tell him. 'The word you're after is *coincidental*.'

I don't believe in coincidence. But what I believe no longer matters. The old man might be all over the shop but I've got to accept what he says and go along with him – otherwise Imogene is going to die.

'*D'accord*, let's not quibble …' The old man's voice tails off as the door opens, and when he speaks again his tone has softened. 'Hello, my darling,' he murmurs.

'Hello, Grandfather,' replies the figure in the doorway.

'Josephine's my other precious granddaughter,' the old man explains. 'And she is a crucial factor in our enterprise.'

She's big and soft-faced and, like Jaqui, in her forties. She's wearing an aqua-coloured uniform with a white collar, and her blonde hair's crammed into a white nurse's cap. After double-kissing the old soldier and Jaqui – who has returned downstairs – Josephine positions herself next to her sister.

'Josephine works in the – castle.'

I note the hesitation. There's a lot the old man's not telling me and a glance at the sisters confirms it.

The nurse's face is pale and Jaqui's eyes won't meet mine. She's staring at her grandfather but addressing me when she whispers, 'The castle's owned by a family that's the closest thing France still possesses to royalty. Nobody likes them. They're snobs. They ...'

The old man glares her into silence before returning abruptly to me.

'*Where* this terrible business is conducted has always been a closely-guarded secret. I know because I have my spies, while Josephine only knows because she works there. Very few others – including quite clearly Jaqui here – know what goes on in the castle. The aristocrats are behind it, as they are behind everything. Their philosophy's the same as that of The Organ Grinders – that is, that some people are better than others, and deserve to live while others can die. The two groups – the aristocrats and the organ-exchange people – are natural bedfellows, which is why –'

The old man shuts up as the old couple, Harold and Maud, drift down the stairs, smiling uncertainly around at everyone before disappearing out the door. Not until the door closes behind them does the old man resume his discourse.

'Who are *they*, for instance?' he asks as their footsteps recede along the street. 'And what are they doing here?'

'They say they're pilgrims,' I tell him.

He shakes his head. And oddly, I get the impression he's shaking it, not at what I just said, but at Jaqui. He turns back to his other granddaughter, the nurse.

'While we're waiting, Josephine, please tell Monsieur about the – castle.'

Josephine hesitates. It must be a family trait, this hesitating.

'All of it?'

The old man frowns at her. 'Just what he *needs* to know.'

The nurse might be discussing organ grinding but that doesn't mean she minces her words. Yes, the operations take place in the castle. The relevant wing of the – again the hesitation – Hôpital Grand Château contains three sections – Storage, Dissection and Transplant.

'We nurses view it as being like a body possessing three primary organs, with the corridors as its veins and arteries.'

She's suddenly even more hesitant, like she fears someone might contradict her. But no-one does. The old man's fielding phone calls while Jaqui's eyes are fixed on the photo on the wall. Josephine seems troubled but continues anyway. Like the other locals who work there, she goes on, she's confined to the so-called *good* section: Transplant. No-one acknowledges the other two sections. Organs appear as if by magic, after which the nurses help the surgeon to transplant them.

'Oh, I'm sorry,' she murmurs, glancing at the old man. 'There's a fourth section – Live Transplant. Of course, no locals work there either.'

'Do you know *when* … I mean *who* …'

I can't utter the words but Josephine knows what I'm trying to say.

'Grandpa trained me to observe,' she says quietly. 'That's why I always check.' She pauses and glances across at me. 'Could you give me a name?'

I tell her *Simon Peter*. Then, in response to her non-knowing look, add, 'He's a dead dancer.' But she's still unknowing, so I try Janus King. Still the blank look.

'Also known as Vladimir Gregorovich.'

'Ah, Gregorovich,' the nurse murmurs. In the semi-darkness, her fingers tangle in her blonde hair like she's trying to remember the proprietary name of a medicine but can only come up with the generic. She glances at the old man and when he nods she continues.

'There is a Gregorovich on our list, but the first name is Natalie, not Vladimir. A little girl desperately in need of a good heart to replace her bad one, the faulty heart she was born with. Not to mention several other organs which ...'

She needs a prompt and I provide it.

'You use the word *desperately*. Does that mean –' I can't bring myself to say it. It's a long while before the nurse answers my non-question. Like an artery, time can stretch until it seems like it's going to burst, only it doesn't. I finally manage, 'Has she had her operation yet?'

'The little girl was waiting for a match but I understand she's no longer waiting. The match must be your daughter. And I understand the operation will be tonight.'

I play it rough. It's the only way.

'Understandings can lead to misunderstandings, so which is it: not tonight Josephine – or tonight?'

After a final glance at her grandfather, Josephine nods.

'Tonight.'

Chapter 37

OLD SOLDIERS NEVER DIE ...

At her words, the photo on the wall seems to turn three-dimensional, as if the young men want to leap into action because their war has restarted. Jaqui grips her sister's arm while Damnation takes hold of mine. Jaqui's staring at me with what looks like mute appeal while the nurse seems to be having trouble continuing. I sense her hesitation and so does the old man.

'Have you checked the surgeon's log?' he asks Josephine.

Josephine nods.

'That's what you trained me to do, Grandpa.'

'Then tell him what it says.'

Her eyes fix on the photograph on the wall behind the old man, like she might find comfort there. 'I'm not scheduled to assist in the operation because it's what's called a simultaneous transfer. That's when they remove organs from one live patient and insert them in another ...'

The old man's voice cuts across Josephine's, 'How do they perform this transfer?'

Josephine takes courage from his intrepidness. But her voice is a whisper so I've got to strain to hear what she's saying. 'The surgeon removes the organ or organs while the donor's still alive. A simultaneous transfer enhances the chance of success because ...'

Her voice fades to nothing but the old man's remorseless.

'Does the log give the time?'

'Twelve-thirty tonight. The donor's death will occur upon removal of the spare part.'

I force myself to speak.

'Which part – which organ?'

'The heart.'

'Then we can get on with the plan,' the old man says, 'in the full knowledge our friend here is in command of all the relevant facts. The troops will be here soon.'

'What troops?' I ask.

It's like he's been expecting the question ever since France's General de Gaulle disbanded his beloved Resistance. 'You Australians have a saying – *Old soldiers never die, they just fade away*. Well, here we don't die either. But neither do we fade away. Instead, we take a leaf out of these people's book. In other words we perform a transplant.'

Jaqui seems anxious to absolve herself of something. It could be guilt.

'What Grandpa means is –'

'What I'm *saying*,' the old man interrupts, 'is that the Grafted Bush – as we now call ourselves – has gone on recruiting. There are a couple of us old ones left, but mainly they are all new, young ones. The new men are taught to shoot and to hunt ...'

I remember the soldiers I saw from the train, near the château, like they were practising for something.

'Above all, they learn about explosives. So we're ready for any threat.'

'Or any excuse?'

The old man glances at me, sharply.

'I see it more as an *opportunity*, Monsieur. And in answer to your next question – just as I recognise that opportunity, I'm more than ready to grasp it.'

'But *why* are you doing this?'

A tap at the door relieves the old man of the need to reply.

Chapter 38

... THEY JUST FIND ANOTHER WAR

One by one the new recruits enter, crushing into the small room between me, Damnation, the two sisters and Le Patron.

'Thank you,' the old man says, turning to the last arrival, an old man like himself. 'Especially you, Philippe, because I know how hard it is for you to get around these days.'

Philippe nods. He looks even older and more decrepit than Le Patron, and appears to be struggling for breath. But his comrade's already moved on to the others – big, raw-boned farmboys, pimply clerks, an academic or two from the local university.

'Tonight's the night,' he says. 'And, pardon my Shakespeare: *Screw your courage to the sticking place!*'

One of the sisters – I think it's Jaqui – has lit a candle. The old man surveys the room in its dim illumination.

'Welcome to Operation Clawheart.' He holds up a hand for silence. 'Don't cheer – the walls have ears. This might be the time for action but it's also the time for discretion.'

'But who's the enemy? Who are we fighting? And what's the target?'

The old man glares the interjector – a young man who seems a lot smarter than the others – into silence.

'You're too young to understand, Martin. Suffice to say, the enemy's the same one it's always been. We needn't go into that. All you need to know is that body vultures are at work in Beguine. What you *don't* know is where they're operating. Well, I can tell you now because it's tonight's target.' He pauses for effect. 'It's the castle.'

Surprise greets his words. Only Philippe, as if he's suspected all along, stays silent. Someone – again I think it's Jaqui, like she's having trouble keeping still, like something's bothering her – has cleared the table, enabling the old man to spread out a map.

'We're going to rescue this man's daughter from the body snatchers. But at the same time we will blitz the joint so it cannot happen again.' He glares around. 'Anyone who doesn't want to take part must speak up now.'

Martin relapses into silence, staring at his hands while Le Patron nods.

I make like I want to speak but Le Patron gestures me into silence. Like any good commander he knows his men. This is the new generation of fighters, brought up on the twilit flictures of the killing of Saddam Hussein. They're sick of virtual reality. They want nice, big, fat, *real* explosions. One or two glance in my direction. 'We'll take the blitz,' one of the recruits says.

The old man frowns the speaker into silence.

'You're not being given a choice. You'll follow orders. Now we're limited by two factors – the balance of opposing forces and the consequences of our actions.'

It's as though someone – it must be Martin – has distracted the old man, causing him to use terms that belong only in a textbook. He quickly corrects himself like he's redirecting an errant missile.

'As I said, this man' – he indicates me – 'wants his daughter back. Plus, as I understand it, his ex-wife. This is our chance to show an outsider what we can do. We have to get it right. First, we need to evacuate the innocents.' He spreads his hands. 'Because, unlike the enemy, we're not in the business of random slaughter.'

I want to argue. I'm not here to blow up castles. I just want to save Imogene.

He jabs an arthritic finger at a few faint red lines on the old map.

'These are tunnels into the château and they're our points of entry. We will form into four teams. I'll lead the bomb squad. Jacques will lead the rescue team. Martin will be in charge of the guards. The fourth group will go to Transplant, where this man's daughter is. They'll be led by Philippe here, with the girl's father and Mademoiselle Dalmation along to make the necessary identification.'

Josephine interrupts. 'The child might require attention,' she says falteringly, like she's not sure what she's asking but might be expected to ask it. 'Therefore, I should be with –' she indicates me '– this man.'

The old man shakes his head vehemently.

'A definite *No* to that.'

'Au contraire, Grandpa – it must be a definite *Yes*.'

'I said no! Those are my orders, Josephine, and you will obey them. If not, you must stay behind with Jaqui.'

'Very well, I will accompany you.' There's a strength in the nurse that's unexpected. 'I will be there.'

'Very well. But you will stay by my side at all times. And after we have set the bombs, you will return with me.'

'Very well, Grandpa.'

As Le Patron barks his orders, there's something else on my mind. When I snap out of my reverie he's already checking an ancient timepiece.

'All right, men, synchronise your watches. It is now 10 pm. H-Hour– that is, the time of the assault – will be midnight.' He turns to me. 'And in response to your earlier question as to why I'm doing this. It is because, Monsieur, we are fathers together, you and I, isn't that so?'

When we arrive at the château, the Ferret's gun's in my pocket next to the lock banger. Everyone with the exception of Le Patron, Philippe and Josephine has come on foot. Le Patron's parking the BSA motorbike nose-out in a bramble bush, steadying the machine while Josephine alights from the back and Philippe gets out of the sidecar. Then – with the aid of a walking stick and with Josephine trotting

obediently by his side – he limps in the direction
of the bomb unit, which is already at work in the
shadow of the château. Even as I watch, I see the
nurse slip from Le Patron's side and scramble down
the hill towards us. Le Patron's too absorbed in the
bomb-laying to notice while Philippe appears too
old to notice anything much at all. As she joins us,
the nurse nods without speaking while Damnation
grips my hand. We huddle at the tunnel entrance
while, several paces away, I hear the young man
Martin murmuring to his handful of guards.
Somewhere in the distance the rotors of a helicopter
start up. Outside the tunnel, we get down on our
hands and knees and the old man's boot moves
against my skull, followed by an urgently croaked,
'Go! Go! Go!'

Chapter 39

THE RED HERRING

A sign at the tunnel mouth reads: UNSAFE ACCESS. Crouching, I follow Philippe. Behind me is Damnation, followed by the nurse. Pick-and-shovel squads have cleared away the bushes that have successfully hidden the tunnel for seventy years. Philippe's cracked voice filters back through the dust. 'The limestone's stable but a cave-in's always possible. Stay close. We don't want to rescue the wrong boy.'

'Girl,' I correct him. 'We're rescuing a girl.'

It's as if he doesn't hear. But it doesn't matter. Just as I find myself thinking and talking like an accountant, I weigh our chances and gauge the tunnel with the mind of a bean counter. The tunnel measures a metre by a metre. There are no struts, no timberwork, no supporting structure as far as I can see. I spit out the lime dust kicked up by Philippe. Time and again I find myself bumping into his boots, hearing him gasp for air before moving on.

Some vague thought's niggling at me, only I can't place it. It's as if all my detecting facilities have been replaced by the accountant I turned into when I put on these clothes. At first I put it down to my childhood fear of confined spaces, courtesy of the schoolyard bullies that locked me in sports bins. But it's not just that. It's more to do with these two old men – the madman that's leading us and the geezer gasping for air just ahead. Plus the memory of that odd, halting interplay between Le Patron and his granddaughters back at the Butterfly House ...

We inch forward in a silence broken only by the clatter of falling scree, its shards scratching my hands, the scrabbling of Damnation and the nurse behind me, and the ragged, laboured breathing of the old man ahead. There's little air. At times it feels like there's none at all. The walls of the tunnel close in. Like the old man, I start to struggle for breath. I stop to wipe the lime-greased sweat from my eyes and by the dim light shed by my headlamp, I check the time.

12.11 am.

They'll operate on Imogene first – cutting the arteries and slicing around the tissue to remove her heart and placing it in a dish of ice. There's to be no life-support system – it's not intended that she live. After they remove the recipient's defective heart, tying off the arteries and placing her on an artificial fibrillator before preparing the chest cavity, Imogene's heart will be –

If Josephine was telling the truth, it's only seventeen minutes to the operation. If ... I damn Le Patron for not scheduling our run earlier. We're in danger of being too late. I wish ... Then I hear Rube saying, *If wishes were dishes*, and fight back my fear. It's too late for recriminations. Le Patron's done his best, hasn't he? But will it be enough? The hill seems

to crumble and the limestone turn to dust while all
hope of saving Imogene seems to be turning to dust
with it. If Josephine was telling the truth … I shake
my head and my head bumps against a boot. That's
when I realise the old man's no longer moving.

'Hurry up!' I shout. 'For God's sake, man, get a
move on, will you!' But his boot dangles immobile
in the torchlight. 'Move!' I shout again. His boot's a
sclerotic lump in an old artery, blocking circulation.
I fight for breath. A voice wavers behind me, beyond
Damnation, falteringly.

'What's happening?'

'I think he's dead.'

But there's no think about it. Death is a profound
stillness and Philippe is profoundly still.

'This is a bad sign!' Josephine cries.

The voice reaches me as if from a distance, like a
stray thought in the mind of an amnesiac. Terror
plunges me into darkness and it takes an act of will
to come back from it, to realise the nurse's voice is
high-pitched and hysterical as she screams that
something's a bad sign. But if Philippe's death's a
bad sign, what's it a bad sign of …?

It's then that the elusive memory – no, *three*
elusive but interconnected memories – cease to be
elusive any more. It's the word *sign* that launches
the process, making me sweat even more than I
am already. The first memory is of the *signs* in the
hospital when I was looking for the Ferret. One

sign read: *Transplant. Not down there,* Damnation said: *It's this way.* The second memory is of Jaqui saying: *His wife – my grandmother – was killed by the Germans because of Le Patron,* in retaliation for his activities in the war. And the third memory is of Le Patron's passionate denunciation of privilege: *Just like aristocrats or the Germans in the war, these people will stop at nothing ...*

This is not about Imogene at all.

How can it be?

Imogene's not even here.

'The time!' I shout back to the nurse. 'Did you give me the right time? Or did you lie about that, too?'

I don't hear her reply. It could be because my fear has shut out all sound. I just manage to hear Damnation relaying the nurse's answer.

'She says the castle was a red herring: the old man wanted to blow up the castle and he also wanted you out of the way. It's because he doesn't want what happened to his wife to happen to Jaqui and Josephine. He's working for –'

I cut across her, 'But if Imogene's not here, where is she?'

I hear the murmur of question and answer behind me, then Damnation saying, 'In the *real* hospital.'

My heart sinks and with it all hope. My sight blurs but I manage to read the time on my watch and – still accountant-like – do the necessary subtraction and addition. Only eight minutes to go. We're in the wrong place at the wrong time. I'm tangled in my fear and Philippe's feet. The feet are stopping me moving. But I must move for Imogene's sake. I yell out, 'Tell Josephine to head back!'

They move and I move with them. Le Patron went to elaborate lengths to fool me. *A final warning,* he said before we left, looking me straight in the eye. *When you get to the end of the tunnel, you'll find the door opens towards you. It's a strategy dating from the time of the ancient Greeks, making fortresses that much harder to break into.*

A red herring, a sop to Sir Boris as Rory would say, a totally irrelevant detail meant to mislead. It was never intended we save Imogene. The old man just wanted to save his girls and at the same time blow up the hated castle. And now, if Josephine has at least told the truth about the time of the operation, it's only seven minutes before they remove Imogene's heart.

Desperation and lime dust turn my tears to paste as Damnation and Josephine shuffle behind me and I shuffle as fast as I can back after them.

Chapter 40

INTO THE VALLEY OF DEATH

Around the side of the hill, the silhouettes of toiling figures are outlined against the night sky. I hear the sound of heavy, homemade artillery being moved into position and the urgent commands of Le Patron.

'We're not going to make it!' Damnation whispers. 'It took us a long time to get here from the hospital, remember.'

'But we were on foot then.'

The motorbike's still where Le Patron left it, the glint of its handlebars and the glimmer of its paintwork barely visible through the bushes. One of Martin's men is on guard but he's distracted by the bomb layers and softly whistling the French national anthem. I cut him off mid-whistle, finding the appropriate pressure point, pressing it, and afterwards helping him down to the ground. The handlebars are cold. The key's in the ignition but I don't use it to start the bike. There are helmets – old, black, dull-painted affairs – but we're not using them, either. I wheel the bike into position. Someone's coming towards us.

'Damnation, get astride the petrol tank. Josephine,

you're in the sidecar. Let's go!'

Clutch-starting a pre-war BSA with two dames aboard is no stroll in the vineyard. I put it into third, raise the valve lifter and push. Someone starts shouting. I depress the valve lifter. The Sloper's engine catches, dies, catches, dies and catches as the bike lurches down the hill. The front wheel twists and the bike threatens to fishtail but I manage to wrestle it straight. From behind us come more shouts. Martin and his guards are almost on us – I feel a hand clawing at my coat – as the engine rattles into life. I thrust away the hand and leap aboard, straddling Damnation, while giving the engine as much throttle as I can find.

The bike twists and turns as the engine splutters, roars, dies, roars again. The old man wanted Josephine out of the way before the bombs went off. She'll be out of the way all right, but not in the way the old man intended. He wanted me gone so he could satisfy his masters, the transplant people. Beyond the running feet I can hear him shouting. But he's not shouting at us. He's ordering the bomb layers to get on with the job. He must have decided that Josephine's safe and is making the best of a bad job. The guards' shouting fades and the running feet fall back. I glance behind as I manoeuvre the bike onto the road.

As our speed increases, my accountant's brain calculates that, despite the load, we're capable of achieving something like 60 kilometres an hour. My suit coat flaps like the wings of Samothrace and the night wind freezes my shaven head. Damnation's soft against me while the moonlight illuminates the balled-up paper by the foxhole we occupied earlier in the day. The engine hammers, the racket echoing into the valley as we head for the hospital, the sidecar bouncing like it's attached to the bike by rubber bands while our single yellow light probes the darkness like a scalpel. I twist sideways, shouting so the nurse can hear me.

'You've got three minutes to tell me everything, Josephine! And this time make it the truth!'

Grandpa made her do it, she tells me. He didn't want – wouldn't allow – what happened to his beloved wife to happen to her and Jaqui. In the war he fought *against* the Germans and as a result of his activities his wife – their grandmother – had died. But he was smarter now. Now he worked *for* the enemy. He was in charge of the transplant people's security.

Which was how he'd known of my arrival. When I turned up at Beguine he suspected that I must be one of the organisation's hunters and gatherers. A suspicion that was confirmed by my arrival at the Butterfly House. He knew he couldn't trust the people he worked for. They could still abduct his precious girls if they weren't happy with him, or even remove their organs if someone offered enough … He hated aristocrats as much as – perhaps more than – the body farmers. So he decided to kill two birds with one stone. Blowing up the castle meant the end of a much-hated symbol as well as the death of any aristocrats who happened to be there at the time. With the help of police and politicians the organisation bribed he might even have got away with it. As for the bomb layers, they were only following orders. They wouldn't know what it was all about anyway. And my involvement would distract me from the real centre of operations while also ensuring my death. And meanwhile Le Patron would win favour with the enemy – which was the whole point of the exercise. And unlike his wife, his precious girls would be safe.

Josephine's voice is sober.

'You and Hélène were supposed to die in the blast while old Philippe was expendable. I wasn't meant to be with you. Grandpa was to bring me safely back on his bike. But I – couldn't abandon you, knowing what I knew. After all, I'm a nurse. But until Philippe died I didn't know what to do. I decided my dying would somehow atone for my part in the death of your daughter …'

Then Philippe died and the nurse saw his death as a sign. As we bump along the potholed road, she's clearly distressed.

'And my daughter?' I demand, my eyes watering with the combined effects of the headwind and the fear we'll be too late. 'What was supposed to happen to her?'

The answer's a long time coming. What did my old mate Harry Hopman like to say? That there are no winners in this world, only losers, and all anyone can do is attempt to limit their losses. 'This is a story about fathers and daughters, isn't it?' Her words are clear because she needs to get across what she's saying. 'Gregorovich is a father and it was your daughter's life or that of his daughter. His daughter needed a heart and your daughter had one. It was the same with Grandpa. He'd lost his wife but he still had us. And he was trying to protect us in the only way he knew how.'

We've reached the valley floor. The clouds seem to be hung out to dry and the river's gleaming in the moonlight. The clatter of the bike is all-pervasive as the hospital looms. Guards peel from the doors and sprint up the road towards us, the moonlight glinting on dull-painted barrels. It's no longer Le Patron's ragtag-and-bobtail group of recruits. These men are professionals, their weapons F1-Famas bugle assault-rifles, modified for nightwork.

'Stop or we'll shoot!'

'Hang on!' I yell to my passengers.

The impact should have derailed us but they made these machines from good old British steel. There are a lot of screams as we smash through the doors. Bodies bounce away from us and the glass shatters into spring-storm raindrops as the bike crashes through.

'The corridor! We won't fit!' Damnation shouts.

'We'll fit all right! Hospital corridors are wide enough to turn a bed in!'

As we skid to a stop, I twist to confront Josephine, who's still occupying the sidecar.

'Where are they? Are they on the floor that doesn't exist?'

Viewed from the outside, the number of hospital floors never added up. I've been thinking like an accountant and all the signs suggested the hospital had four storeys while my eyes insisted there were five.

Josephine nods and I aim the bike for the lift. But a sign says *En Panne* – Out of Order.

'I forgot – they decommission the lift when they …'

I don't wait for her to finish.

'Fire stairs?'

She shakes her head. 'They lock the door to the fire stairs at such times.'

It's a heavy-duty door with steel reinforcing, built to resist most forces. But the bike's built that way, too. I ram the gear selector into First and twist the hand-throttle for the run-up. The corridor's not only wide enough to turn a bed in, it can take a lot of bike, too. I straighten the machine and bring the old 500cc engine up to its full 3000 revs.

'Stand back!' I yell.

Damnation dives to one side as I unleash the clutch. There's a bit of nonsense as the wheels look for purchase and we're sideways-on to the direction I want us to go when the tyres finally grip. The motor's screams ricochet off the walls and the sidecar becomes a Catherine wheel as it gets tangled up with a fire extinguisher. The building shudders as the BSA makes contact with the door, over which a sign shows a little green man running up a set of stairs accompanied by the words *FIRE ESCAPE*.

The bike rams into a concrete step and a sharp pain rips through my leg. I'm dazed as Damnation hurries towards me, followed by Josephine. It hurts but I manage to stagger to my feet. The bike's opened the fire door part of the way. I shove it the rest of the way. The stairs lead to the floor that's not there …

'Give me a hand!'

I'll need them – the nurse anyway. For the kid, if

not for me. The two women prop me, one on each side, as I drag my disabled leg up the stairs. The last door is what Le Patron said we'd find in the tunnel.

'It opens towards us!' Josephine yells. 'But it can't be locked from the inside because of fire regulations so it's open!'

The door leads to a high, wide corridor on the fifth floor, the level that doesn't exist. There are no more signs. Just the corridor and too many doors. I glance at Josephine.

'Which door?'

'I've never done a simultaneous transfer.' I'm prepared to believe that much at least is true. 'But I've done the other operations.' She points shakily. 'So, by a process of elimination, behind that door is your daughter.'

She's indicating a door at the end. I hesitate, nursing my shattered leg. We can't afford to get it wrong now, there's not enough time.

'We're down to the wire, Josephine. Are you sure?'

'Yes,' she assures me. 'They do their operations one at a time,' she goes on as she helps me along. 'We're talking millions of euros per procedure. It's not an assembly line – it doesn't have to be. They only do one operation a night. They're here all right.'

We head along the corridor, Damnation on one side and the nurse on the other. A faint sound of music emerges through the door.

'The door's pretty well soundproof,' Josephine whispers. 'They take every precaution. And it'll be locked.'

'Stand back!'

I bring out the lock killer, place it against the

keyhole and the explosion's no more than a rat's squeak.

As I push open the door and we go in, we're hit by a blast of music.

Chapter 41

DANCING WITH BRICKS

We find ourselves in a room behind a high, wide insul-screen featuring a lot of little Beatrix Potter rabbits disporting themselves in a garden that – the screen, not the garden – muffles any noise we make upon entry. That and the music. No-one appears to have noticed us, anyway. Beyond the screen, I count five figures – three female, two male – wearing plastic gloves, shoe covers and surgical masks. A sixth is curled on a bed. And in the far corner a seventh stands slight and shadowy, closely attending to what's happening under the harsh arc lamp, under which lies a small, still shape, raised high on the operating-table as if for sacrifice.

And always the music. Over which booms a voice.

'Mehr narkose, Herr Anästhesist!'

'He's speaking German,' Josephine murmurs beside me. 'Grandpa made me learn German, it was one of his obsessions. The surgeon's German and he's asking for more anaesthetic, which means ...'

But she doesn't need to tell me what it means – either the words or their significance. I know German. I also know the figure on the operating table's Imogene.

'Not that it matters as far as the donor's concerned,' the surgeon continues, shouting to be heard over the music. 'But an anaesthetic gives us a happier heart.'

I'd been expecting French, because this is whatsisname: Green, Serge Lifar, Lover Boy – the man with the hands. Nosey Nora said he was French. And Aunt Rube agreed. After all, Rube decided the word on the tape was *Merde!* But Rube wasn't her usual self – instead she was looking for easy answers when there never are. The word wasn't *Merde!*

I also recognise the music. It's Tchaikovsky again but this time it's his *1812 Overture* – the one with all the cannons going off at the end. I slip off my coat and hand it to Damnation, setting the screen rocking as I do so. Somehow above the music the surgeon hears the screen rocking. If the music was any louder I could wear it as a coat, yet Lifar heard the screen rocking.

'What was that? Don't you morons realise that – apart from the music – I require absolute silence?'

It's an assistant's job to reassure and an assistant reassures. But Lifar isn't satisfied. He demands someone check for the source of the noise. Footsteps approach and an aqua-coloured gown stops on the other side of the screen. The figure comes no closer – it mustn't be in the contract to peer around screens. But the nurse is close enough for me to assess her rate of respiration. It's a long way from normal.

'It's nothing, doctor.'

'But I tell you I heard something!'

That's when a third voice – one with a heavy accent

– interposes. It's Russian – more specifically one of the six Slavonic languages, possibly Ukrainian. I identify the speaker as Gregorovich, the father of the recipient, the dancer who agreed that my daughter would make a suitable donor when Lifar produced her for inspection.

'What are you, Lifar, some kind of prima donna? This isn't ballet, you know. You're a defrocked morphine dropkick who lost his licence and I'm paying you a fortune to do a job. Now do what that fortune entitles me to and remove the heart.'

'But to do that I require peace and quiet.'

'You have a lot better than that, Lifar – you have the music of a great Russian composer. Remove the heart.'

In awkward counterpoint to the crash of cymbals, someone starts singing. I recognise the voice as that of the surgeon. The addict tremor is pronounced. Despite the language, I recognise the song. The surgeon's sub-conscious has kicked in and the result's not pretty.

'Gott sei dank fur kleines Mades ...'

'He's using regional German,' Josephine whispers. '*Mades* is another word for *Mädchen* – it means little girls! He's singing ...'

The word on the tape was *Mades*, not *Merde* ...

Up to now I've been reluctant to move. I was worried I might hurt Imogene. I was in the kind of nightmare where all will is stripped away, as if some all-powerful force pinioned my arms, a nightmare I couldn't wake from.

Damnation's got my coat while Josephine's checking the upside-down dial of her nurse's watch.

And when the nurse looks up and her eyes meet mine, the eyes are appealing. She crooks a finger at me, indicating half. Thirty seconds to deadline.

As I hobble around the screen I hear the father cry out in anguish: *Nyet! Nyet!* But it's him or me, his daughter or mine. And it's *my* daughter's heart. I forget my leg, go down hard on my good one, and leap across the operating theatre.

There's a moment — the briefest of nanoseconds — when the surgeon, blade in hand, stands, wide-apart eyes staring out of the handsome face familiar from the photograph. It's like he's seeing what he once saw in his drug-fuelled hallucinations. He tries to get out of the way but he's too late. Bone crunches against bone as my heel catches him full in the face and his head jerks backwards. The surgical assistants scatter in a pale-green blur as the scalpel clatters to the parquet. Lifar lies still. He's no longer singing.

Josephine's suddenly beside me. I push her. 'See to Imogene!' I yell. She moves but I've been distracted. Damnation calls out from the screen, 'Look out!'

I go into the half-pirouette, using the good leg to take all my weight. On the turn I find the Russian in centre stage. He's abandoned his attempts at English and is swearing above the music in his native Ukrainian. I sink to the half-crouch but the dancer's lithe figure follows mine. It's like we're linked by the piano wire of a garrotter. Before I can move again, Gregorovich pauses to gather up the scalpel. The blade flickers in his hand and the eyes in the broad Ukrainian skull fix on mine like a snake's.

He's no longer dancing to save his daughter. With the surgeon dead, she's no longer got any hope of a new life from that quarter. He's acting out of unrequited hope, dancing for vengeance. I see it in the forward thrust of his body and in the way he's holding the knife. He comes at me high and wide with his head back, legs together and arms spread. I've got nowhere to go. As the dancer's arm slices down, I'm hampered by the corpse of the surgeon behind me, the tray of instruments on one side, the nurse leaning over Imogene on the other, and my bad leg.

I'm a body in the making, and if a dancer knows anything, it's body language …

Chapter 42

DANSE MACABRE

I smell the stifling stench of disinfectant and the thick, galling odour of anaesthetic, feel my body crushed in a dust-filled tunnel to nowhere, blinking in the half-light, tasting what I think must be limestone until I recognise the bitter-sweet bile as the dancer descends. All in slow motion, as if time's stopped. Fine dancers can do that and Gregorovich is a fine dancer. With the music hammering in the background, I try to shield my daughter by standing between her and the dancer, awaiting the death stroke. It's all I can do. But it's not all Josephine can do.

Uttering a strangled half-cry, she spins from the operating table as the death dealer descends, interposing her big body between mine and the dancer's. Their combined weight thrusts me onto the surgeon as – above and beyond the music – a shot rings out. I'm expecting the knife of death. Instead the dancer's doing the puppet dance from *Petrushka*, arms flailing, body twisting, legs jerking, head thrust back as he soars for an instant above me before finally crashing down.

The knife plunges, but not into me. Josephine's

big, heavy body sags against mine and lies still. And on top of her, the dancer Gregorovich is no longer moving. Past them both, I make out the figure of Damnation, my dark-grey accountant's coat crumpled beside her, Parisian jeans-clad legs wide apart, arms extended in front of her. And gripped in her two fists is the gun that once belonged to the Ferret.

I try to extract myself from the tangle of bodies but can't. I need to check on the kid but the bodies and the bad leg prevent me. My sight blurs and I hear a roaring in my ears. At first I think it's the cannons in the music only it's too soon for the cannons … Damnation knew where the gun was, the Manurhin MR73, .357 Magnum that was in my pocket. She also knew her way around the coat because she's been there before. It was simply a matter of … But how did she know how to fire the thing …?

One of the bodies moves. It's Josephine. Someone's still alive in this mess and it's the nurse. But looking at the blood leaking from her, I know she won't be alive for long. She wasn't the target, she just made herself that way. I settle her on the floor, cradling her head in my arms.

'Is your daughter …?' she whispers.

I nod.

'She would have been safe if I'd told the truth,' she murmurs. 'You could have got here in – plenty of time.' She tries to raise herself but falls back. 'Don't be hard on Grandpa. He made me lie but it was only because he didn't want what happened to his wife to happen to me and Jaqui. So this time he was on the side of the enemy. He wanted to protect us even if it meant putting your daughter in the firing line.'

Her fading eyes seek mine.

'Ironic, isn't it?' I don't correct her because she doesn't need correcting. 'Grandpa sold his soul to the Devil in order to protect us. Yet I'm going to die because of it.'

'You'll be all right.'

Josephine manages a pain-racked smile. 'It's nice of you to say so, only it's – not true. It's like the lies I told you. In the end my lies cost me my life and it looks like your daughter has gone the same way …' Her voice wavers as she sags in my arms. 'Even more ironically, someone could have had my organs but now there's no-one here to …'

Her voice fades and I feel something within me fade with her. I'm lowering her down to the floor when, above the racket of the Tchaikovsky, I hear a crash and look up in time to see a group of men with blackened faces explode into the operating theatre. And far off, in some twilit world beyond the music, as consciousness leaves me, I hear a series of explosions.

Chapter 43

THROUGH A GLASS, DARKLY

Strong hands pinion me. I panic as I feel a needle enter my arm. Immediately afterwards – or it could be days or even weeks – I hear the clatter of what might be helicopter blades. Or maybe it's just the music. There are more explosions and I nod to myself. It must be the music. The music must be helping the replacement surgeon as he attempts to bring Imogene back to life …

I struggle but shadows fall around me. To the east – it must be the east because that's where the sun rises, even in France – I make out the glow of a beautiful dawn heralding the promise of a new day.

Followed by darkness.

'Careful!'

And dimly, as if from a great distance, the same voice, 'What do we do with him now?'

It could be a dream, a dream in which words make a half-sense that's worse than no sense at all. I sense a logic but it's the logic of *Alice in Wonderland*.

Shapes approach and recede. The voice is soft yet it batters my soul. The words make a great deal of sense yet they make no sense at all … But it's not a sunrise, it's the castle. Le Patron has achieved one of his crazy aims, he's destroyed the château. Below – it must be far below, the drugs have warped my perception of distance – the castle's no more than a series of scattered fires and piles of dust. Le Patron thought I'd be there, that in killing me he could make amends for the death of his wife by saving his granddaughters. He was only half-right. Jaqui might be alive but Le Patron's efforts have resulted in the death of Josephine.

That's irony.

My mother was a drug-crazed madwoman who wanted to take me – her five-year-old son – on a roundabout-ride to death. But in the end she took only my sister because I hid, hearing her croon as I did so: *Come to me, my little rainbow, Rainbow by name, rainbow by nature, come to me …* At a fair I was given a toy after failing to hook seaweed out of a horse trough. The toy was a kaleidoscope – a small, tube-like affair which showed pretty much what my mother saw when she gave birth: a rainbow. Me and my sister thought we could see a magical future in that explosion of colour – the gyrating circles, the refracting and diffracting spectra. We believed we were seeing the Utopia that our parents ranted on about. We decided it was our own special angel's portent, as if the future might bring us a wondrous beauty, instead of … My mother dead.

My sister dead.

And now my only daughter …

But when I became a man, I put away childish things.

For now we see through a glass, darkly.

What I see now through the fog of whatever they injected me with is another flash of multi-coloured light – the goddess Aurora spilling dew upon the earth to bring life to all things. But there's no life here, no wonder or wisdom and little joy. Instead, rocks and bodies spew into the early morning sky and the flames are hellfire. I feel the helicopter pitch and shudder, rise and fall and rise again. I struggle but my heart isn't in it. I've lost my daughter. I feel the jab of another needle followed quickly by another and the pain in my leg fades. And for a long time after that, all I see, hear, feel and experience is nothing. Nothing at all.

The chopper is more stable now and I'm grateful for that. I try to open my eyes but something's forcing them shut. Cramp gnaws at my guts like hungry rats. I struggle to remember the significance of rats, but like everything else on the edge of my consciousness it eludes me.

Amnesia is an anaesthetic. They must have injected me with amnesia.

The helicopter's falling from the sky and my guts lurch and my eyes swim. A voice orders me to fasten my seatbelt. I hear the scream of engines and feel the chopper pitch and shudder. The leg's hurting again, my mouth's dry, I can't open my eyes and my gut's been chewed to pieces by rats.

I'm in a wheelchair trundling along a walkway. The air's cold, much colder than it ought to be. I run a hand over my skull. No hair. No hat, either. I must have left the hat in the tunnel along with … What tunnel? I remember a body blocking my way and the words of the nurse, followed by the terrible realisation that –

I must be somewhere in France yet the voices around me aren't French. And dimly through those non-French voices I hear a small, reed-thin one saying, *'He's waking. Get out of the way and let me wipe his eyes, they're full of gunk …'*

And I know I'm dreaming because it's Imogene's voice and yet Imogene's dead.

Chapter 44

THE KID IN THE QUEUE

Fingers gouge into my corneas and water dribbles under the collar of my shirt. I force my eyes open and a familiar face swims into my vision like an image refracted in a goldfish bowl. I'm a goldfish. Because, while I'm opening and closing my mouth and saying nothing, the human outside the bowl is speaking. And the image and words make no sense, no sense at all … *You're not who you think you are. You're not Mister Rainbow but Norman Halliwell and you're returning from – where?'*

It's a test. I can do tests. Rube taught me how to do tests. I concentrate on my answer.

'France,' I hear myself say. *'I'm returning from France.'*

'Correct. And what is your name?'

'I am Norman Halliwell. I am a bald accountant and my name is Norman Halliwell.'

I turn to face the man in uniform checking my face against something I can't see hidden behind his counter. I rub my hand over my head again. Someone's reshaven my skull. What else have they done? But I can't wonder about that. I've got my work cut out just remembering who I am. Because

I've given Norman Halliwell not only my heart but also my body. Norman Halliwell exists because I brought him back to life. Norman Halliwell is me, I am Norman Halliwell. The man in uniform looks like a grinning satyr as he gives me back the passport, the one with someone else's photo in it.

'I note from our files that you left Australia hale and healthy, Mr Halliwell. Yet you've come back in a wheelchair. Are you sure you're who you say you are?'

It might be an attempt at a joke but I'm not laughing.

Anyone can see I'm not myself.

'Where's your luggage?' Customs wants to know.

'There's no luggage,' Damnation replies. 'It must have been mislaid en route.'

As we pass out into the free world, I crane my bald head to see who's pushing me. And suddenly I'm in the tunnel again and unable to breathe again. Because the person pushing my chair looks like Imogene.

'Who are you?' I ask.

'Come on, Daddy!'

'You're Imogene,' I whisper.

'Right! And for that you get a tot of vodka.'

Damnation told me later that Imogene wouldn't let anyone else near me. She even had a little joke about it – that if anyone was pushing her father around it was going to be her. She laughed as she said it – laughed because she's Imogene, laughed because she's happy, laughed because she could, because she's alive.

She who lives last, laughs best.

'Come to Mummy, darling.'

It can't be but it is. The dream was a nightmare that turned into real life then back into a nightmare again. Salina must have been the figure on the bed in the operating theatre, lining up to have her organs extracted as an add-on extra after they'd finished with Imogene. And now she's walking next to Imogene like nothing ever happened – not a marriage, not the birth of a daughter, no divorce, no wild-eyed escapade to France in which Imogene nearly lost her life, not even any happy returns. I feel the grip on the chair handles tighten.

'I can't. Because right now I'm looking after Daddy.'

Imogene plonks the chair at the head of the taxi queue like it belongs there and I recall that when you're disabled, even in Sydney, you go to the front of the queue. Other memories come back, too …

'What happened to the dancer's daughter?'

Damnation answers. She's on the other side of the wheelchair from Salina, wearing this year's Parisian chic and looking as beautiful as ever.

'After I shot the dancer in the operating theatre and while you were out to it – they had to give you injection after injection because you thought

Imogene was dead, and apart from that were in great pain from your leg; were in fact, in my humble opinion, stark, staring mad – I visited the room next door to deliver the bad news to the would-be recipient.'

There's a long wait for a taxi that's configured to take a wheelchair. But this is Sydney.

'*Am I alive now?* the little girl wanted to know,' Damnation continues. '*Daddy promised me I'd be alive after the operation.*' Damnation takes a deep breath. 'I told her, Yes, she was alive but there'd been a bit of a hitch and there had been no operation. The little girl actually looked relieved. *That's good,* she replied. *Daddy said no-one would die giving me organs but I couldn't see how that could be, not when one of the organs was a heart. Was Daddy being true to me?*'

It's my turn to take a deep breath.

'What did you say to that?' I ask.

'I replied that daddies were always true but some daddies were truer than others.'

I have trouble getting my brain around what she's said. 'What happens to the little girl now?'

'She returns to the back of the queue.'

Which we don't have to, because just then a cab with a bubble back arrives. And as Imogene wheels me into it, preparatory to getting into the cab herself, I spot the old couple, Harold and Maud, conversing quietly together at the back of the queue.

Chapter 45

THERE WAS A
CROOKED MAN ...

I stay in the chair in the back of the cab as Sal and the kid decant themselves at 21 Castanet Close, the shack uncurtained and unwelcoming. The kid leans in and asks if I'm all right and I lie through my teeth and tell her yes. After which the hack drives me off and dumps me in Darlinghurst beside a twisted wheelchair ramp cobbled out of old bits of plumber's pipe and splintery scraps of second-hand marine ply. I recognise Rory's handiwork.

Rube answers my Mike Hammer, tugging open the door with a twisted wire coathanger she's affixed for the purpose and for a long while we look at each other from our respective wheelchairs. There's got to be something to say but neither of us can say it, so in the end, Rube lets me in in silence, wheeling herself down the hall ahead of me to the living room.

'Where's the machine?' I ask.

'What machine?'

'The one that was keeping you alive, the kidney pumper with all the bells and whistles.'

Rube chucks me a sly look.

'I no longer need it.'

'Why is that?'

'Because I've got a new kidney.'

'Where did you get a new kidney?'

'From a live donor who was more than willing to …'

'Come on, Rube, I might have a broken leg but –'

'All right, you like clues so I'll give you one: the donor was brain dead.'

'Good old Roarer! So that's why he wasn't at the airport! He's convalescing!'

Aunt Rube's wound must still hurt because when she shrugs she winces.

'It's not good old Roarer at all. I'm grateful for what he did but he didn't do it for me. According to the Knock-Kneed Church of the Born-Again Idiots, donating an organ means you hit the eternal jackpot. Rory might have lost a kidney but, in so doing, he scored a first-class ticket to heaven.'

'Coincidence?'

'No, Rainbow, irony.'

I change the subject. 'How's the boat?'

'As you might say yourself, Rainbow, *Wooden No.* I've been too busy keeping myself afloat to worry about boats.'

I spend a few days with Rube. I don't go into detail about the trip to France, and in return she brings up nothing about me trusting Damnation. Instead, with difficulty because she's in a wheelchair, she makes up a bed on the couch and I go to sleep to the sound of drug addicts screaming at each other and wake to the refrain of traffic. It's good to be home but when Rube reckons I've had enough fun, she kicks me out. On the way she hands me an envelope. I open it on the bus. It's brief and it's in French.

Dear father of the little girl. It was very sad losing both my sister and Grandpa in the one coup. The explosion was terrible. Because he couldn't walk very well, Grandpa couldn't make his getaway without his bike so he went up with the castle. Many others also lost their lives. There is to be no inquiry however. The papers said the explosion was caused by a gas leak. I hope me giving you the warning about Grandpa helped in some way. He was wrong, I know. But in his defence, he believed he was acting for the best. He just wanted to protect us and because we were his granddaughters we had to obey him. He was our Grandpa, after all. I was happy to hear your daughter survived everything. The operations have stopped and now the top floor of the hospital is devoted to the victims of bomb blasts. In closing I am going to marry Martin, the man who put you in the helicopter. He's a good man. Jaqui

I'm out of the chair and we're standing in the Pitt Street mall, a piece of roadway clawed back from Sydney's traffic. I ignore the busker eating fire, focusing instead on Damnation. It's not hard. She admits what I suspected all along – that the entire operation was a fit-up. Flax was hand-in-surgeon's-glove with Lifar. While Lifar acted as spotter, surgeon and general factotem, Flax was the fixer and

Damnation the go-get girl.

She pauses, emotion rendering her momentarily breathless, leaving me to fill in the gaps.

'Your friend Lifar spotted Imogene,' I say, 'befriended Salina, then paraded Imogene before Gregorovich, who approved of her as a donor. Lifar arranged a medical for Imogene to ensure compatibility. Lifar then focused on getting Imogene and Salina out of the country – the organisation deciding they could use the mother's organs as well. You agreed to teach them French. Everything was hunky-dory until in a swollen-headed moment – maybe they *were* in a relationship – Gregorovich blabbed the story to Simon. Which made Simon a threat that had to be eliminated.'

She holds up her hands like she's trying to ward off the truth.

'Honestly, I – I didn't know what they were up to. To me it seemed to be something – oh, I don't know – exciting. I didn't know it involved abducting and killing people. I just thought – Oh, I don't know what I thought. I just felt it was – well, *romantic* being a little bit on the wrong side of the law.'

My new hat's too big because I'm anticipating hair regrowth so it wobbles when I shake my head.

'Except there's no such thing as being a *little bit* on the wrong side of the law, Damnation.' The eyes are still beautiful and she's still gorgeous but something's changed – it must be the eyes of the beholder. 'After we arrived in Paris you kept Lifar informed of our movements – I discovered that from your call log. You took me for a ride but somewhere along the line you changed your mind and tried to change trains.'

Damnation gazes at me sadly out of her no-longer-so-sloe eyes, like she knows what's coming.

'I – I fell in love.'

I let it pass. You've got to let a lot of things pass in this game.

'Okay, so while you're still in love tell me this: was it Flax that duffed the dancer?'

After the briefest of pauses, the dame nods. She's in truth-telling mode and it hurts.

'When Simon became a threat, Lifar gave Albert the job of – eliminating him. I didn't know at the time – I only worked it out afterwards.' She pauses. 'Remember my telling you Albert was an ex-Olympian? Well, it was the truth – he was a gold-medal marksman who didn't mind getting his hands dirty. His father was a politician. Two of the tickets were meant for Albert and me. Lifar bought a third – the child's one – but that was just a red herring: he always intended cancelling it. But your daughter must have guessed it might be significant so …'

So Imogene hid the ticket in her music box, along with the mini recorder. Beside us the busker survives his ordeal by fire, and the crowd chucks a few coins in his cap.

'So Flax attended the ballet to deal with the dancer that knew too much,' I say. 'But wait on – you and Flax were in the dress circle and it was a loge shot.'

The dame shrugs. 'Albert told me he needed to stretch his legs. It's something old people do.'

'What – shoot people?'

'No, stretch their legs.'

I let it pass, along with the foot traffic.

'And when Flax returned after stretching his legs, did you ask where he'd stretched them?'

Damnation shakes her beautiful head.

'Albert paid my bills. I didn't want to upset him by asking too many questions.'

'Talking of shots, you had your place shot up, didn't you? In order to look like you needed my help. The shooter was in the room when he took the shot when I was there, exiting by the window afterwards. I know because the broken glass was *outside* the house instead of inside. That was Flax, too, wasn't it?'

'Look, I can explain ...'

'Where is he now?'

Damnation's face indicates sadness.

'He had a stroke when he heard what happened. He left everything he had to some political group in memory of his father.'

It's peak hour and the sky's a glowering masterpiece over the heads of people scurrying to work in order to earn enough money to return to work tomorrow. You might be able to make sense of it, I can't. I start in the direction of Circular Quay but Damnation follows me.

'Please, I only knew what I needed to know! There was a lot they didn't tell me. The helicopters at the hospital, for instance – one of which Jaqui's friend Martin commandeered for us to escape in. I didn't know about them or anything else, really. I was in my own little compartment, like you and me on the train ...'

The busker's doused his flame and it's like the fire's gone out in me, too. I watch the crowd disperse. There's something familiar about the busker. But he couldn't be the same person. That was Paris and this is Sydney and besides, Proteus is dead. I turn back to Damnation.

'You even told them I'd worked out the beggar was with them. That's why you dropped your phone in the toilet, so I couldn't see who you'd called. But after you dumped your phone you couldn't call anyone any more. And then there was the major clue that you were on their side – when the Ferret killed the concierge, he left you alive.'

'But it's not what you think,' she cries. 'Not in the end anyway. Oh, Rainbow, I fell for you and I've still fallen for you. Which is why I helped you, don't you see? I switched. I worked out what *GREEN* meant, didn't I? And I was able to kill Gregorovich because Albert had taught me how to handle guns. Everything came out all right in the end, didn't it?'

I'm back to the old non-identity, together with the old clobber – pink jacket, yellow-spotted shirt and whitesides – and somehow it feels right. I'm my old non-self again and I'm thinking again. I doff the new fedora.

'See you round, Damnation,' I say.

She's standing stock-still as the busker departs and I continue on to the wharf, the lemmings scampering around me.

'But you won't, will you?' I hear her reply, faintly. Or maybe she didn't say anything at all. Perhaps it's no more than the murmur of too many soles clattering on the footpath. I catch a glimpse of her reflection in a shop window as I make my way up Pitt Street, an island of loneliness in a sea of commuters.

Chapter 46

BULLETS AT THE BALLET

When he telephones – I don't ask how he got my number – I pass what Damnation said on to Ace Mollema. Ace says he knew about Flax, which confirms my suspicion that he knew a great deal all along. I bring up the matter of Harold and Maud.

'Look, Rainbow, mate ...' he begins.

'Don't *mate* me, *mate*. I was set up by Damnation and the body farmers. But it was a set-up by you as well, wasn't it? So you could use your old mate Rainbow – the kid that once saved your life – to do your dirty work and break up a body-parts ring at the *minor* risk of killing my daughter.'

'Come on, Rainbow, you're too suspicious. All right, so I might have organised a couple of late cancellations so you and your lady friend could make that flight to France. But I promise that the man in black, the beggar and the gunman on the train were on the other side. We only added the old couple to the mix for your protection. But I'm not hearing any thanks for that.' Mollema simulates being hard done by. 'For God's sake, Rainbow, Harold and Maud saved your life in the Louvre. I could have abandoned you with no protection at all. I –'

I interrupt his self-justification.

'In which case, you wouldn't have got your result. You needed me alive, Mollema. And while you were safely back here, my kid was at the pointy end of a killer op. Harold and Maud were instructed to protect me, and also to get me to Jaqui's place so I could make contact with that madman, Le Patron. For all I know, you could have organised my daughter's abduction as well.'

'Jesus, mate, credit me with a little –'

But I'm not crediting Mollema with anything, other than a lot of guile and total bastardry. If I was still Halliwell, with recourse to an add-up book, he'd occupy nothing but the debit column. I might be paranoid but I've got a lot to be paranoid about. It's called survival.

'Feel free to contact me if you need anything,' I hear him say.

I click him off and chuck the dead-man's mobile in the Harbour.

Last time I was at the Opera House they put on a tragedy. But tonight's different. For a start the Bullets at the Ballet case is done and dusted. And for a finish I'm here with Imogene. She's wearing a neat little pale-green number with her hair pulled back, making her look far too grown-up in my opinion. But I don't care how she looks, I'm just happy she's alive.

'I'll have a champagne, please, Daddy,' she says,

looking around at the other ballet goers. 'And make it Moët' – she says it right: moh-ette – 'I believe it's the most expensive drink they have.'

I do like she says even though I shouldn't, and when she takes the glass she doesn't slop it, which is more than I don't do with my beer.

'I guess this is the appropriate time to ask you the question, Immo. Why did you hide the ticket?'

She smiles over her expensive champagne.

'You taught me to beware of Greeks bearing gifts, Daddy, and all by myself I decided that might extend to other nationalities as well. I figured the ballet ticket might be important and I decided I was right when Lifar became very angry when he couldn't find it.'

'And the mini recorder?'

'It had one word on it that would help identify Lifar, regional German for "little girl". How was I to know you'd think he was saying something else?'

'How old are you, Immo?'

'Old enough not to take nonsense from you any more, Daddy, even if you did save my life.' She sips her champagne and when she hands back the glass it's empty. 'Now, let's go in, shall we?'

I haven't had time to read the programme but it doesn't matter with ballet. All I need to know is that, as we listen to the band do its knees-up, I feel for the first time in a long while that it's nice to be alive. And as the lights go down and the darkness closes around us I also get the feeling that Imogene's safe – at least for the duration of the performance.

But that's before the gun goes off.

It's a whipcrack of a sound. I'm thinking Colt .45

– one of the long-barrelled ones – or maybe a Smith & Wesson .38. At the second *crack!* I make a dive for Imogene. It's an awkward move due to the crook leg and the seats, so I'm a little less balanced than I'd like to be. The music rises to a crescendo as I drag Immo down between the seats while the ushers make a beeline in our direction. Imogene takes a round-arm swipe at me – accidental or otherwise, and I suspect it's otherwise – as she struggles to her feet.

'What on earth are you doing?' she demands.

'A gun went off! Don't say you didn't hear it?'

Imogene shakes her head.

'Daddy, a gun was *supposed* to go off. The ballet's *Mayerling* and in *Mayerling* guns go off in every act. The ballet's about this aristocrat who –'

But the ushers are almost on us so I grab the kid and shove her in the direction of the exit.

'Fill me in on the details later, Immo. Because right now we've got to make ourselves scarcer than a legitimate body part.'

The kid goes quiet and I cover my scant regrowth with the new fedora as we leave. In a nearby concert hall someone's churning out Tchaikovsky's *B-Flat Piano Concerto*, and as I hobble past I hear them working themselves up to the fast bit, where the music goes into overdrive. And if you can't hear the menace behind the music, you haven't been listening.

Also in the series

978-1-922057-20-4 (digital)
978-1-922057-45-7 (print)

Winner of silver in the 2012 Independent Publishers Awards.

She's a surgeon, she's beautiful and she desperately wants
Mister Rainbow to shed some light on her husband's past.
But when he does, she wishes he hadn't. Because what Rainbow
discovers is a handless hood — and a whole lot of murders.

Rainbow's a retro private eye who keeps himself to himself.
He lives (illegally) on a boat in Sydney Harbour, has no identity,
and frequents speakeasies. He's also got a nemesis called Pandora …

The Case of the Hood With No Hands is the first novel in the
sensational Mister Rainbow heptalogy.

Also in the series

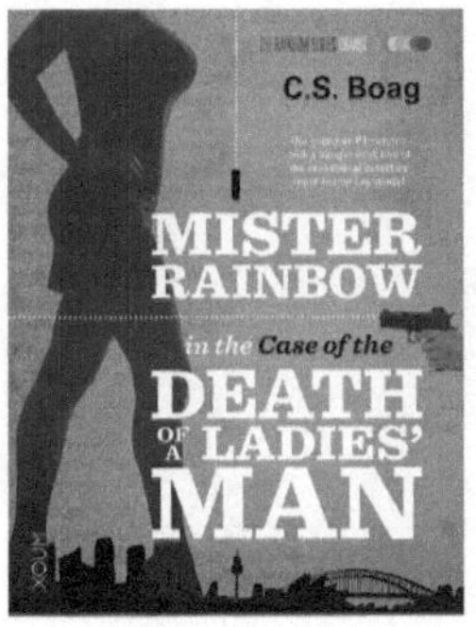

978-1-922057-53-2 (digital)
978-1-922057-54-9 (print)

When Mister Rainbow finds a headless honcho in a Kings Cross alleyway, the tattoo around the corpse's neck leaves little doubt as to its identity. Thomas L. Tycho was everybody's enemy – a trickster, a dirty dealer, and a wide boy who made the mistake of wide boys the world over – not making himself narrower when the gun went off.

The killer's identity, however, proves more elusive – as everybody hated Tommy, anybody could have popped him. His wife, his girlfriend, and half of Sydney's underworld all had motive, but Mister Rainbow smells something fishier than usual, and it's got nothing to do with what's floating in the harbour …

The Case of the Death of a Ladies' Man is the second novel in the sensational Mister Rainbow heptalogy.

Also in the series

978-1-922057-67-9 (digital)
978-1-922057-68-6 (print)

When a few too many dead bodies turn up on Sydney's mean streets, Mister Rainbow's too busy to investigate – until an old flame goes up in smoke.

Then it's no holds barred as the famous PI with the dancing feet finds himself pitted against the city's crooked gamblers – and the dame determined to whip them into line …

The Case of the Horses for Corpses is the third novel in the sensational Mister Rainbow heptalogy.